JONATHAN PRYCE and

The Magic Stone

JONATHAN PRYCE and

The Magic Stone

TEMPLE PRINCE

CS Crystal Spectrum Publications, LLC
Asheville, North Carolina

Library of Congress Cataloging-in-Publication Data

Jonathan Pryce and the Magic Stone/ Temple Prince
pages cm

LCCN 2015955413
ISBN 978-0-9911532-2-0

Printed in the United States

Published by

CS Crystal Spectrum Publications, LLC
Asheville, North Carolina
www.crystalspectrumpublications.com

Dedicated to Jeff

Whose Steadfast Love
has offered Support and Encouragement
Throughout the Years

TABLE OF CONTENTS

Chapter One, A Find 1

Chapter Two, The Cave 11

Chapter Three, Inhabitants 21

Chapter Four, The Chamber of Souls 31

Chapter Five, The Last Battle 37

Chapter Six, Magda and Amara 47

Chapter Seven, Training 59

Chapter Eight, Battle with the Grygots 69

Chapter Nince, Kaz 75

Chapter Ten, Transfiguration 81

Chapter Eleven, Home Again 87

TEMPLE PRINCE

One

A Find

"Victory!"

Jon whooped as he thundered down a low rise along a worn path through the field by his house heading toward the woods. A large dog bounded near his heels. As they flew through waist high weeds and bobbing wildflowers, branches from small scratchy bushes slapped at their bodies and snatched at the dog's shaggy golden fur. Jon flopped on the wide grassy bank under a great old shady maple tree by the stream at the edge of their property. He sucked in big gulps of air and mulled over the events of the past few hours.

"Victory…at last!" He threw his right arm into the air in triumph. "Yeah!"

Jon placed his hand over his racing heart, a heart that had not slowed since he burst through the red, white, and blue banner strung taut across the finish line. No–one showed more surprise than him when he finished in first place in the six hundred–meter run in Wellington Junior High School's final track meet of the season. This meet included three other schools with top–notch track teams. His full season of practice and competition had finally paid off!

"Stasos, I won! I won!"

He flung his arms around the thick neck of the frisky dog and buried his sweaty forehead into long soft fur. Stasos returned the attention by straddling Jon's body and licking congratulations over Jon's face with a big sloppy tongue.

As he leaned back on both elbows, Jon replayed each second of the race from the pop of the starting gun to the moment his chest touched the finish line banner. Two things stood out from the jumble of images. First, his mother's smile and laughter, something he had missed for a long time. Second, the shock on Brett Thompson's face as Jon sprinted past him into the lead. Jon liked Brett. But Brett reveled in competition and almost always won the meets. Not a kind winner, he enjoyed beating down other runners including his teammates. "Second–rate, always late," still troubled Jon's ears from early in the season.

What changed this time? Jon wasn't sure he *could* win. Brett oozed 'champion' from every pore. His confidence and size provided an edge, especially in the longer races. He had grown tall this past year. His stride had lengthened and his body's muscles had bulked up. In comparison, Jon's arms and legs remained thin and spindly. Jon wanted to be tall and strong like his dad. But when he looked in the mirror, his mother's expressive eyes and angular features stared back at him. He shared her straight untamable sandy hair. The girls at school called it dishwater blonde. He cropped it short now for track season. Overall, he looked more artistic than athletic.

Now, what was it? This race was different. And a last chance to score a victory for at least another full season. *Last and final chance of the year.* His entire family stood at the sidelines. They cheered so loud, they embarrassed him—especially Andrea.

He mostly yearned to see his mother without that stamped–on anxious look, just for a few minutes. He wanted to win—for her. He had to win for her he thought as he forced himself into a faster rhythm during the race. Stretching each foot far beyond the other, he fixed his concentration on his feet. Foot, then foot, then foot, then foot. His long sure stride exploded into a rapid rhythm. He pushed his pace until pain threatened to buckle his legs. At that point, Jon spotted Brett in the lead by a half a meter.

Then the world slowed into a blur. Jon glided forward as if he were floating. He passed Brett on the outside and increased his lead. He broke through the finish line banner with arms flung back and chest bowed out. A blur of bright colors and noisy cheers swirled around him as he hunched over with hands on both knees to catch his breath.

His mother's light hair stood out from the crowd. She laughed! She actually laughed! She was clapping, jumping, and hugging Andrea. His father threw him a thumbs up.

Brett finished second and way behind him. Brett stood there and stared as if Jon had popped him in the face.

When Coach Coleman yelled at Brett, "Shake hands," Brett stuck a couple limp sweaty fingers in Jon's palm and slunk away never saying a word.

A gusty breeze ruffled Jon's hair and brought his attention back to the present. He tugged off his socks and cross trainers to wade into the cool water of a shallow pool near the stream's edge. Then, cupping water in his hands, he let it drizzle over his flushed red face. Stasos sniffed around in the taller grass on the bank with great concentration tail wagging. *I'm not the only one excited*, Jon thought. He leaned over, dug out a flat smooth stone from the creek bed, and spun it across the water's surface.

"One," he counted out loud as it skipped. It plunked into the water. The next stone flipped from his fingertips.

"One, two, three," as the next stone skittered across the quiet water. It made the three–quarter mark across the stream's width and disappeared into a circle of translucent water spiders skimming over the surface.

That's better. He reached into the sun–kissed water for the next volunteer. With its wet smooth edges at right angles between his thumb and forefinger, he curled the medium–sized stone toward his body to start the spin. His arm straightened and then stiffened in mid-toss.

What? How unusual!

He held the shining chunk at eye level. The sun glinted from tiny opalescent crystals embedded in the flat side. Salmon and gray colored flecks formed fine lines crossing the surface. Jon ran his index finger over the irregular ridges on the edge. *Curious shape.*

He hopped back to the bank and sprawled out over the spiky grass while holding the rock before him.

Strange! I've never seen these minerals.

Vague patterns emerged from the contrasting crystals before they disappeared back into a jumble of texture. And the stone grew brighter as it dried. Bright sparkles flashed the sun into his eyes making him blink. *How interesting! History made today!* This rock was destined to be the greatest prize of his rock collection!

Jon grabbed his shoes and raced back toward the house. His mom and dad both appreciated nature. Wait until they saw this!

He cut through his mother's prized vegetable garden and navigated around the staked tomato plants, taking care not to injure a single leaf. With one big thud, he leapt onto the wide planks of the generous porch that framed the front of their large log home.

His mother, visible through the screen door, bustled as she placed the dinner plates on the table for supper. She squeezed her brow into tight furrows. Her eyes looked far away.

Nancy Pryce never noticed Jon's noisy leap onto the porch. She brushed long bangs away from her eyes as she pondered how to approach her husband regarding this new house problem. She knew he'd insist on taking action to protect the family, perhaps finding other accommodations for a while. *What a depressing thought!* She loved this house. They had moved out of town away from the university over a year ago and built their big timber frame home in the woods of the foothills after an exhaustive search to find a few fine acres of country property. With mature trees just right for a tree swing, a mountain stream for wading, and an open level plot for her garden, they had found this perfect place to raise their family. The house and land together created a dream come true. She spent many satisfied hours working the soil of her lush vegetable garden and fine-tuning the placement of her flowerbeds. The first of her summer flowers were beginning to break out from colorful buds. She would not miss those spring blooms!

Jules, in his meticulous engineering manner, had planned the layout of the rooms and, the house functioned well. However, problems had started when the septic tank leaked. After that, long legal battles followed with the contractor, and now, this.

The kitchen door burst open.

"Mom, I found the best rock in Summit County!"

Nancy beamed at him, and after a quick look, her face collapsed into instant disapproval.

"Jonathan Pryce! Look at your feet. There is mud *all over* them. Go get cleaned up for supper. And where is Stasos? I hope you didn't leave him down by the creek again. If he comes back in the same condition as the last time you will be the one responsible for brushing him out and giving him a bath." She underscored this last part with a nod of her head and raised eyebrows.

Yep. That's mom—business as usual.

He stepped outside and washed his feet under the spigot.

"Stasos" he yelled toward the creek.

Stasos's big brown eyes and snout emerged from the weeds almost instantly. The Golden Retriever's real name was Athanasios as christened by Jon's mother because she adored Greek culture and art. She had said, "This fabulous dog needs a dignified and valiant name."

They rescued the bleeding pup from a ditch along the roadside one frigid sleeting winter day—an obvious hit and run. Jules had wrapped the weak dog in an old blanket and lifted him into the back of the car. After a quick trip to the vet, the entire family cheerfully took turns nursing him back to health at home. While the hip and hind leg healed, Jon made a few weak–hearted attempts to find an owner by posting "Dog Found" posters around town.

No–one claimed the dog. With a sneaky smile Jules finally admitted, "I guess we'll just have to adopt him ourselves."

The pup turned out to be everybody's best friend. Jules nicknamed him Stasos, and that name stuck because it was easier to say than Athanasios. Especially since Andrea had peeped, "Athansassesses" and everyone shrieked with laughter every time she said it.

During supper Jon tried to show his parents his new find, but their excitement over the race prevented any other discussion.

"You know I talked to Brett's mother for a minute after the race," his mother confided between bites of vegetarian lasagna. "She said she never thought you had much oomph. She couldn't believe someone beat Brettie. It's about time he learned how to be a good sport."

His dad's bemused stare suggested that something else was rifling through that massive brain.

One person wanted to see his new stone—way too much.

"Hey neat, Jon," Andrea squealed. She tried to snatch the stone from his clenched fingers. "Let me see that!"

"No way!"

She clutched it in a death grip and Jon bent her fingers back to wrest it away. She hollered. A tug–of–war began. She didn't let it rest. She let out a piercing wail when he pushed her back. Her screech could alert the entire city of New York in an emergency.

"That's enough," Jules put his hands flat on the table. "This is not acceptable behavior. You both need quiet time. In your rooms."

In his bedroom, Jon lay on a fuzzy brown rug and flicked bits of lint onto the wood floor. He and Andy often fought. Deep inside he knew he liked her, but she was such an irritating pest. He couldn't control himself when she bugged him. She was always getting him in trouble with his parents with her big mouth and screeching, even for a slight jab. His parents expected him to be the sensible one since he was five years older and ought to know how to behave. He wished they would take his side one time. He could hear Andrea in her room, playing the radio and singing in her squeaky little voice to Stasos. Some quiet time!

Nan's strained voice filtered through his slightly ajar bedroom door. She kept her voice pitched low.

"Jules, it happened again this morning while the children were in school. Now I don't want to alarm anyone but I'm becoming somewhat concerned. If it gets any worse we may have to leave the house."

Jon interpreted her last comment as a smart tactic, like heading the horses off at the pass. If she mentioned leaving first, his dad would offer the opposite idea to try to calm her.

"Each time it goes longer and stronger. Today the dishes rattled so hard they almost fell out of the cabinet and, Stasos howled off and on for an *hour*."

His dad tried to sound reassuring.

"Now N–N–Nan, take it easy. The builder has agreed to come up here first thing Monday morning to search for *any* flaws in our foundation. There is no history of earthquakes around here. I have no idea what might cause all this movement."

Their voices faded off, and Jon found himself in a dream. Sparkles similar to the crystals on his new stone filled the sky and air. He sat and rocked gently in a tiny boat—to and fro, to and fro, rhythmically in a wooden boat. An oar dipped into twinkling water sprinkled sprays of stardust over the boat. Jon smiled as he dipped in the other oar and laughed as those sparkles settled onto the water. They created swirling patterns over the surface.

The swirling sparkles formed a picture and, as Jon peered into the water to check the result, the boat lurched forward. His head snapped back, and he bit his tongue. Ouch!

The dream changed. The water churned, and the sparkles turned into tiny razors zipping through the air. They slashed large splinters away from the sides his boat. The darkening water rose with fury. Choppy waves spilled over the sides of the boat and flooded the small craft's bottom. Water poured into the bottom at an alarming rate! His body shook and shivered with terrible unknown dread. He dropped his oars and gripped the boat's wobbling wooden sides. He *must*. Must *what*?

"Jon," came a voice from far away. "Jon".

Someone called his name. His mother. He opened his eyes. The bed was shaking! His entire room—no, the entire *house* was shaking! His mother swooped into the bedroom, grabbed his arm, and jerked him from the bed.

"Hurry! Outside!"

Together, they rushed though the shaking house to the front yard where Jon spotted his father in the glow of the front porch light. Jules stood in a clearing between the woods and the house with chest bared and wearing his favorite old worn striped pajama bottoms. He sheltered Andrea in his arms. Her thin flowered nightgown flapped around her toothpick legs as she clutched her father tight and buried her head into his collarbone. The wind flailed two blonde curls against her eyes. She sobbed so loud Jon was sure she scared away the most of the wild animals near the house.

The four stood in line and watched the quaking house with disbelief. As the surrounding trees waved eerily back and forth, the ground below rippled with the motion of a moving snake. Tree limbs crashed in the deeper woods and the flowerbed that hugged the house morphed into wacky modern art.

Jon watched his mother's mouth drop open as he struggled to maintain his footing. He shifted his balance as the ground veered away then back again. The movement caused flip–flops in Jon's stomach. The family swaggered around the front yard like drunken sailors. Something crashed inside the house and Jon's mother whimpered in duet with Andrea.

At last, the shaking eased. Everything became still and the peeping of frogs from the stream went from a cappella to the full chorus of night sounds. Jules took charge.

"Well that solves one mystery," he stated in his best matter–of–fact voice. "The foundation is as solid as it looks. The quaking is coming from the ground below and *not* the house. Maybe there is a small fault running under here. We'll check it out as soon as possible. But we better try to sleep now."

Noticing their stressed faces, he wrapped his arms around Jon. "First, how would a cup of hot chocolate taste? It might settle us a little."

Jules conducted a quick survey around the house for dangerous cracks while Nancy concocted a quick bedtime snack by preparing small sandwiches and hot chocolate. Jon and Andrea helped by sweeping up a broken cup and plate from the kitchen floor. After that, they piled scattered cookbooks onto the bottom shelf of the large island centered in the kitchen.

The family gathered at the massive oak table to munch their sandwiches. A stifling blanket of silence settled over them punctuated by an occasional chair squeak and Stasos scratching his nails over the wood floor as he tried to make himself comfortable. Eventually they shuffled off to their bedrooms with simple, good nights, to each other.

Once again in his room, Jon remained too much on edge to sleep. After fidgeting with his covers, he picked up his new stone from the bedside stand. He excavated a big old magnifying glass from under a pile of clean socks in his dresser drawer. The grooves and ridges on the stone's surface formed a familiar pattern. *Hmm, a face. The face of an old man. Am I dreaming or does it glow? Is it looking at me?*

Still uneasy from the evening's strange events, Jon placed the new stone in the far corner of his room to keep it separate from his main collection. Before he fell asleep, he decided to search the creek bed in the morning. Maybe he would find another one of these peculiar stones.

Two

The Cave

The first rays of pleasant Saturday morning light filtered though his window blinds. Jon slid out of bed with joy—no school! He'd be able to devote his entire morning to searching for stones. No need for breakfast. He pulled a long–sleeved tee shirt over his head and slid a pair of old jeans up over his legs. If he woke nosy Andrea, she would be extra baggage on his quest, so he had to move with stealth.

A beaded replica of a Native American deerskin pouch served as a handy tote for his new found stone. He crammed the stone into its bottom. His current rock collection occupied three of his six bedroom shelves and the best samples glistened in every square inch of his windowsill. A neat label punctuated each one with the rock type and its mineral composition if known. Jon had collected the various interesting stones and rocks populating the hillside since the first day they had moved into this house. Rock collecting was a hobby that his science minded father encouraged.

With the leather drawstring pulled tight, Jon tied the colorful pouch on his belt along with his running shoes. He glanced at the door of his parent's silent bedroom and tiptoed through the house. As he passed Andy's room he cracked the door just wide enough to make out her lumpy shape snoring from under the covers. Stasos formed a sleeping mound of fur between her pillows. Jon slipped through the front door with one hand to ease the screen door back to its place, then scampered in his bare feet toward the creek.

Morning fog still hovered in the lower areas. The air hung heavy with the smell of woods and damp soil. Jon savored early morning visits to the stream. He might spot a possum or fox drinking from the pool's edge before they ambled off to their homes to sleep for the day. The raccoons shuffled off with no haste swaying from side to side as if to advertise, "We're not afraid of you."

The water level, fed by the generous spring rains, caressed the upper banks at the deeper sections. Jon launched his search in a shallow section bordered by small boulders. He rolled up his jeans and waded into the water where coolness lapped his ankles.

Around him, water splashed over assorted multihued rocks before it collected into a large pool just off the far bank. The quiet pool mirrored the green shoots that cascaded from the lush overhanging foliage and reflected flyby insects back up to the dawn sky. Last summer Jon swam at this exact spot with his family. They sat on the bank to dry off, and afterwards shared a picnic lunch of small sandwiches, fruit, and cookies. His dad had talked about adding a rope swing to the big maple, but hadn't found time to put it up yet. Now surrounded by bird song, Jon listened to the woods wake up.

He spotted a glint near a large rock off his big toe. A flat rock, roughly the same color as the stone he found the day before, lay nestled between two darker rocks. He pried it out of the sandy creek bottom with a small twig. But, as he pulled it out of the water, he recognized that it was not the same. False alarm.

He fished through the water again and scanned the bottom for nearly an hour before he found anything similar to his unusual stone. The midmorning sun warmed his back through the cotton shirt as he hunched down toward the water to get a closer look. *Let's check this one.* He pried a sparkling flat rock up from the creek bed with his big toe. *Hmm, pretty close match.* He rubbed the rock against his shirt to dry it, then reached into his pouch with his other hand to compare the two side by side.

As soon as the original stone emerged into the light, something unexpected happened! His stone quivered and slipped, or rather, *jumped,* out of his hand. It plunked into the water with a strong splash and floated downstream from his left side.

"Hey!"

He lunged after the fleeing stone.

"Hey!"

Every time he pounced toward it, the stone frog–hopped an arm's length in front of him. Then it bounced into a strong current and swished away in the rapid current impersonating a whitewater raft.

Amazing!

Jon jumped onto the bank and grabbed a long stick caught between some rocks. He raced along the bank trying to block the escapee from moving further.

"What's with you?" he shouted after it. "Stones don't float."

He observed it, but his eyes wouldn't lie, would they? *Maybe it's not a stone.*

He set his determination to recapture his prize. He must have chased the stone a mile before it swerved into a small rock–lined whirlpool. Around and around it whirled. Jon's dizziness grew as he followed it. Then the stone slammed against a larger rock and sprung high into the air. It flew over Jon's head and landed a few feet away, on the nearby bank.

Winded, he sprung at the spot where it now lay still. Then John caught a movement out of the corner of his eye and stopped short.

The source of the movement disappeared but, *what is that?*

Beyond the sandy clearing and, partly hidden in the nearby brush, loomed the entrance to a cave, one he had never noticed before during his long hikes around the hillside. A ring of tan and gray mixed conglomerate formed the mouth and Jon estimated the opening's size as five feet high and three feet wide.

I can get in there! He jumped with excitement.

For a moment, Jon forgot about his stone. He shaded his eyes with one hand and peered inside the opening. The angle of the sunlight lit the scattered rocks of the near interior allowing him easy visibility. The cave promised fun and adventure. *This cave might contain more stones like the one I found!*

Jon fixed one eye on the stone which remained motionless in its sandy depression. He needed a minute to catch his breath, so he sat down on a large rock and stretched his bare feet out to dry in the warm air. With toes tipped up and heels jammed into the sand Jon leaned back to let the sun fall full on his face while he considered the pros and cons of entering the cave. The pros easily won. Untying his shoes from his worn leather belt, he prepared to investigate this fascinating new find.

As soon as he picked up the half–buried stone to push it deep into the pouch the bush beside him rustled. Jon recoiled with one quick hop. The *strangest* little animal leapt out from between the quivering branches and landed on all four of its tiny feet right in front of him. It looked like a snow white weasel with black feet. The weasel and Jon stood still, staring at each other for a moment. Then the creature pivoted half way around and darted into the cave.

Jon's heart thumped. He stepped to the entrance and peered into the cave. The little animal had disappeared.

Do weasels bite people? He wanted to follow the curious animal. He hesitated as he remembered the recent quakes. *Would he be safe in the cave during a quake, possibly facing a frightened weasel?*

He looked around. The warm morning sun shone through a cloudless blue sky and the slight breeze relaxed him. He yearned to investigate the inside of the cave and find that weasel. It appeared safe enough right now. Curiosity dampened his caution. He stepped into the shadow of the cave's mouth.

Jon paused and inhaled dampness as his eyes became adjusted to the reduced light. He heard water trickling somewhere far away. The passage before him widened a little inviting him to tread further into the dimming recess.

Jon worked his way deeper into the cave as he evaded the scattered rocks that peppered the floor. He reached out toward the jagged wall for balance and connected with the softness of the short gray–green moss. It smelled musty, and he sneezed. Then he edged forward to a narrow passageway. He squinted and strained to see through the tunnel ahead.

Where did that weasel go? To his disappointment, it was nowhere to be found.

A nearby cough cracked the stillness. Jon's body tensed. *Was it the weasel? No, someone else!*

Again, "Hack, hack."

The noise, now louder, came from his leather pouch! He pulled at the knotted cord as if a detestable creature clung to his waist. The bag dropped to the hard rocky floor with a soft thud and an irritated, "Ouch!" His stone rolled out, glowing and displaying a disgruntled face.

"Thank the good fates—fresh air!" It gasped. "A malodorous leather pouch is not the most pleasant environment." It wheezed. "This will never work. Send a boy to do a man's work; Jharliss has made a mistake this time."

When it noticed Jon's astonished face, the stone stopped moaning in its hoarse voice. "Oh, excuse me, lad. I believe introductions are in order. My name is Orlo."

"You're a talking rock!" declared Jon not believing his eyes or his ears.

"Brilliant deduction, my dear boy, but not quite accurate. I may appear to be a rock just now, and I'm abiding as a miserable rock essence but, let me assure you, I am positively *not* the metamorphic medium." Orlo spoke with great certainty although in an old–womanish sort of voice.

"Meta what?" Jon asked.

"Rock, boy, rock. I am not a rock."

Jon was curious again, "Then if you're not a talking rock, what are you?"

Orlo paused glancing at Jon from the side of his eye as if he wasn't sure how to explain himself. "Well, er, uh…do you believe in magic Jon? That's what I am now. A little magic."

Was this a trick? And how did it know his name?

"If I didn't believe before I guess I do now." He found no other explanation.

Before Orlo, the magic talking rock, said more, the cave walls shuddered. A great rumbling arose from deep underground and everything vibrated. The rock walls moaned. The tremor intensified to a frenzied shaking.

A quick lurch threw Jon off his feet and he gasped as chunks of mossy rock and dirt whooshed around him and smashed into the walls. Debris pounded his head and shoulders from above. He jumped behind a nearby boulder for protection. Several large rocks rolled straight toward him.

He flung his arms over his head as a shield and turned to run to the mouth of the cave. But he was too late. Not the slightest ray of light showed through the blocked entrance. *Oh no! Trapped!*

He rushed forward and tried to force a large rock aside. Grunting, he pushed with all his might but it remained rooted to the cave floor.

He groaned, "Now, how are we going to get out?"

The quaking stopped. The cave quieted once more, and the

dust settled to Jon's feet. Orlo appeared unconcerned about their predicament.

"You'll be all right," he said. "I know another way out. But first we have more important things to do. And we don't have much time. Kaz will be awake soon. We must hurry along. Jharliss is expecting us. Set me on your shoulder boy. I'll explain as we travel."

Jon's mind raced with questions. *What was this talking magic rock? Who were Kaz and this Jharliss? And how were they going to get out?*

Jon worried about his situation although the stone seemed trustworthy. Besides, he had no alternatives. It was impossible to dig through the rubble around the blocked entrance and he had to get out of there.

Somehow he knew to lift Orlo the talking rock to his shoulder where it locked into his shirt and balanced itself. The stone directed him deeper into the cave.

"That way boy," he said blowing a small stream of steam out of his mouth.

Jon picked his way through the fallen rubble and noticed his clear and easy breathing despite the settling dust from the quake. Stranger still, he saw quite well in the dark.

The stone responded to Jon's thoughts.

"You're surprised at your ability to see in here, eh? Well, I will inform you regarding this special place. You might pass through here again someday. This land lies between the physical world and the nonphysical world. It is a way station between the laws of visible nature and the laws of the unseen forces. It contains qualities of each. You can see now because you've become acclimated. The unseen forces are directing you. However, you'll return to the predominantly physical when you return to your home."

"I'm sorry, I don't quite understand."

The stone explained, "Well, in the Outer World you are limited by your own physical self and that of the Outer World. An unseen part of you is present but its influence is weak. Your last race is a good example. You ran fast in other races but your force of will, for whatever reason, was strong in the last one—strong enough to make you run a little quicker to win the contest. But try to run against the trained bodies of your experienced Olympic Champions. Even strong force of will would not help you there."

Orlo chuckled and went on. "Force of will is more powerful here. It can push your physical body to run with the speed of a gazelle. But to utilize its power, it must be trained, like the physical body does in the Outer world."

How does Orlo know about my race? It must be the magic.

Eager to learn more he asked, "And what is the nonphysical World?"

"Ah…the Inner World. We have not yet passed. There the nonphysical, or unseen force, is strong, and the physical presence is diminished. Actually, it *is* physical," he went on. "But in a different way than your world. You don't have the means to detect it or measure it although, many times you can sense it."

Jon wanted to question the stone more, but Orlo stopped him.

"Prepare to climb. We are reaching the outer chamber."

Indeed, the character of the passageway was changing. Its low ceiling forced Jon to stoop to go forward. He would have turned back had the stone not urged him on. The slope which had been gradual now turned into a steep incline, and Jon reached for some odd looking twisted roots to pull himself up through the tunnel.

"Hang on to me lad. I'm slipping."

Because Orlo's hold on Jon had loosened, Jon found it necessary to carry him. Jon held Orlo with left hand and used his right to work through this cramped section of the tunnel. He shoved his feet into dirt covered roots that formed small stair steps. The ascent proved difficult but, *I must push on*, he thought. *There is nowhere else to go.*

All at once the passage ended, closed by long dangling roots. Jon couldn't go further. *This goes nowhere, and this stone is crazy.*

"Go on. Push your way through those roots and hang on to *me*."

So Jon pushed harder while spreading the roots, then fell through to a stunning cavern beyond his imagination. A forest of sparkling stalactites and stalagmites made of the same iridescent stone as Orlo spread out before him. Dense patches of cloudy mist lay scattered among the towering rocks and reflected hues of brilliant greens, golds, blues, salmons, and silver.

"How beautiful!" he gasped. Ahead Jon heard the unmistakable sound of water splashing and running.

"The River of Deeds," The stone answered Jon's thoughts again. "We'll cross it before we meet Jharliss."

"Who is Jharliss?" asked Jon getting confused. He thought they were looking for an exit.

"My twin, although she doesn't look much like me now. She is expecting us soon. Ferret has announced us."

"Ferret? You mean that little weasel animal I saw run in here?"

"Black–footed ferret," Orlo corrected. "Her kind is almost extinct. She can be trusted most of the time, but what a ride she gave me upstream! She must have dropped me at least ten times. I'm lucky I wasn't worn down to a little pebble by the time you found me."

Orlo rambled on. "But she and Jharliss and I make a good team. We have done an outstanding job taking care of this place so far."

An alarming new thought crept into Jon's mind.

"Am I dead?" he asked almost in a whisper. "Did I die in that quake?"

"Oh no, no, no, no, no. Rest assured, you are as alive as you ever were. In fact, I might say you are more alive now. You have greater access to your mental faculties."

The stone's smile reassured Jon.

Orlo clipped his words and his face grew grim.

"Trouble coming." He lowered his voice to a bare whisper. "We don't want them to know we're here yet. We had better conceal ourselves."

Three

Inhabitants

Orlo puffed out a cloudy line directing Jon to a nearby crevice. "Sit in there. Remain still and silent until they pass,"

Puzzled, Jon followed Orlo's instructions and pasted himself into the back of the crevice against the unforgiving rock wall. He sank into a crouch and set Orlo on his knee. Orlo blew out a slow steady stream of fog. It wasn't long before the fog surrounded them with a thick reflective cloud.

A faint clicking noise gave way to a loud clattering. Jon shifted his weight and strained to glimpse the origin of this racket through the cloudiness that hid them.

"Be still," Orlo said in a stern yet hushed voice that caused a knot in Jon's stomach.

A shape scuttled out into a thin patch in the dense fogginess. Orlo no longer had to worry about Jon's smallest movement. He froze into a perfect statue as large, dark spidery creatures with ratlike heads emerged from a foggy patch and proceeded in single file toward them. Click, click. Clickity–click, click. Ferocious spidery bodies under segmented dark shells clacked when they walked. Their shells erupted in spiky armor plating over plump abdomens and sturdy legs. Small deep–set eyes darted back and forth as if they were scouting. They moved with jerky and irregular motions.

One menacing face paused before Jon's crevice allowing a closer view. Its black pinpointed pupils widened and contracted as its beady eyes scanned the surroundings. Jon held his breath as twenty of the creatures moved on their eight long clackity legs past his hiding place. Their size matched his!

A small mouse darted out from a crack in the opposite rock. In an instant, a rodent head snapped forward, caught, and crushed the unfortunate creature in its toothy jaws. Blood spurted out over its nearby companions. Like sharks in a feeding frenzy, they squealed with excitement and scrambled over each other trying to lap up the drops.

Jon held back a wave of nausea as he studied the cruel faces. He shuddered. One of them opened its mouth to reveal long yellow pointed teeth covered with clotting blood. A sense of danger penetrated Jon to his core, to be replaced by an aura of rottenness that pervaded this entire place.

The last one scraped the rock wall with its hard shell next to Jon's hiding place. Jon shrank back as its head pivoted in his direction. It halted. He caught his breath. His heart wanted to leap out of his chest. The creature's mean eyes passed across the front of the crevice. *It's looking for something.* Then it turned to catch the back end of procession trailing into the fog. Jon froze back into his statue pose and concealed himself in the crevice for what seemed like forever as the racket faded into the distance. He wanted to go home! Back to his familiar room, his school, his parents, and even bratty Andrea. And what was that thing he sensed. *Something is wrong here. Something bad is about to happen.* How did he know this? He just knew.

"It's all right, Jon, the grygots are gone." Orlo spoke in low quiet tones with an edge of care. "Let us go now, too. Quickly!"

Jon followed a path toward the gurgling river. Orlo perched again on his shoulder. The pathway, composed of level packed dirt, made traveling easy and the trail lay soft underfoot. Short walls of rock alternated with tall walls and formed a border along the sides of the path. The short wall underscored wonderful panoramic vistas in the enormous cavern but this time the remarkable beauty went unnoticed. Although protected by the enclosing wall, Jon kept looking for more grygots. *What if they return?*

Ahead the path widened to form a larger opening and revealed a small circle of land. A group stood in the clearing. They weren't grygots. He sighed with relief. As they approached the gathering, Jon discovered they were tiny little people—men, women, and children—leprechauns or elves or munchkins or something! Little people similar to those in his schoolbook stories. Their height ended at his knee. Tears streaked the children's faces. The adults tried to comfort the littlest ones. The group gave scant attention to Jon as he drew near, but one of the little men bowed to Orlo.

"Greetings sir," he sniffed. He wore a moss green tunic with pieces of dried leaves sewn into a decorative geometric pattern at the hem. Tight green pants and brown fur–lined boots with a chip of sparkling rock at the toe finished his outfit. He pressed a small leaf cap to his chest under a grizzled face and a curly brown beard streaked with gray.

Orlo nodded to him. "What happened Reil?" he asked.

"They got one of the little 'uns' pet mini–bunny sir. It panicked and slipped out of our hiding place. There weren't enough of us 'ere to give 'em a decent fight. It was brutal. They tore it apart first. And then they fought over the pieces. It was almost as if they knew we watched. It was all we could do to keep the children from giving us away."

They must mean the grygots, thought Jon remembering the bloody teeth.

Orlo locked a steady eye on the children.

"Be at peace," he said. "Mini–Bunn has passed to the Inner World. She is safe and happy now."

"Yes, the Inner World," echoed the little ones.

"I will have Jharliss chant for her," Orlo offered.

"Thank you, sir," said Reil. "The uptick of these disturbing quakes bothers everyone. They destroyed our house twice, ya know."

While Reil struggled to compose himself, he glanced in Jon's direction.

Orlo said, "Reil, meet Jon, our new friend from the Outer World."

The group repeated, "Outer World," with wide eyes and the little ones whispered and pointed at Jon. Jon nodded.

"Jon, meet Reil McBain and the Keepers of the Bridge."

Orlo explained to Reil, "Jon will help us with Kaz, and now we must be on our way. Jharliss is waiting."

The Keepers bowed to Orlo and then to Jon.

Reil warned, "Be careful at the bridge, sir. It's weakened from the quakes and we haven't been able to repair it yet due to the extra work needed on our homes."

"Thank–you, Reil," said Orlo as both he and Jon returned the bows. Then they turned away from the group and headed toward the River of Deeds.

Far below in a secluded chamber, lay something monstrous…ominous. A team of sentry grygots waited nearby, ready to act as informants and aides for their malevolent master when the time came. Rank breath emanated from two hideous nostrils as the monster lay sleeping. It reveled in demonic dreams and happy memories—The Black Death, a wonderful time in existence, manipulating ignorant and superstitious men into acts of depravity—or horrible holocausts from ages past still kept secret from the mass of humankind.

It fed on and enjoyed any bit of negativity and fear. Sometimes in its wakening state, the monster stirred. A pointed fin flapped or a clawed leg brushed against the chamber walls and the cavern erupted in a series of shocks as the rock itself recoiled from the touch. The excited grygots sparred and tore at each other in restless anticipation of the coming destruction. Soon.

As Jon trudged along, the volume of gurgling water increased. *The river must be close!* The surrounding atmosphere buffeted his body with several unusual sensations. He sensed timelessness here and another indescribable oddity, being near a hole in space, but somewhere neutral, neither good nor evil. A strong earthiness came over him, feeling like he stepped into his own physical body for the first time, as if gravity itself had gotten stronger. He stretched out his arms and flexed his fingers to test his increased body weight. They drooped with heaviness and it was an effort to keep them extended. Full of questions, Jon glanced at Orlo, who snoozed on his shoulder and appeared peaceful. Jon decided not to wake him.

Rounding a curve in the path Jon was astonished to see not one, but two rivers. Each disappeared into different chambers a good distance beyond to his left. The rivers displayed different characteristics. The first, smooth like moving glass, glimmered with an internal light like fireflies in the dusk. The second, however, frightened Jon. Its water boiled and churned. Jagged, icy–looking chunks floated though a dark gaseous murk. Short whiffs of foul odor pricked his nostrils as the clouded water spurted over a rocky bottom and released puffs of gas and mist.

A narrow wooden footbridge swayed over each river. Short boards, bound together with knotted brown rope, composed the floor of each one. The smooth gray boards formed an even pathway. Between the floorboards the river way below peeked between the cracks. Horizontal ropes strung at different heights parallel to the platform offered a variety of choices for handholds. The bridges' width allowed one person Jon's size to cross at a time, although Jon supposed a group of the Keepers could pass over it three abreast. His path led to the nearest bridge, the one spanning the quiet water.

As Jon stepped onto the first floorboard his strange feelings intensified. A peaceful contentment washed over him. It rose from the smooth water and it invited him to linger at the midpoint of the bridge and absorb the pleasant feelings. The odor of sweet spring flowers showered over him. He walked into the vibration of a soothing tinkling music. *Déjà vu. Where have I heard this before? Sometime, a long time ago.* He ached with happiness to hear those tones again. Orlo shifted and smiled in his sleep.

Jon hurried across a worn stretch of land to the second bridge. A putrid wall of sulfuric stench smacked him in the face as he approached the first board and caused him, coughing, to stop. Orlo snorted and woke up.

"Here already, eh Jon?" he coughed. "Better hurry across before we choke to death. Be careful not to let any of that liquid splash on your body. It is acidic. See what it does to rope?"

Indeed! Acidic gas and liquid had eaten away significant lengths of the twisted fibers composing the rope supports. A few areas sported mere fragments of rope left sagging under the weight of the boards. It looked dangerous.

"Gee, Orlo, do you think it will hold us?"

Orlo didn't reply, and Jon stepped onto the first fragile board. He remembered Reil's words, "Be careful." Then, using short jumps, he tested the bridge's ability to hold him. *Sturdy enough.* Satisfied, he stepped onto each single slat, one foot at a time and shifted his full weight to the next slat as the last held. He looked way ahead to where the bridge ended. It seemed a long way off.

Jon barely reached the midpoint of the second bridge when the cavern emitted an enormous cry and the shaking and rumbling erupted once again. The bridge jerked to his right and the corresponding jolt threw him off balance. He lost his footing and crashed to his knees. Orlo plummeted to the boards from Jon's shoulder perch. They both began an immediate slide toward the edge.

Jon grabbed at the vibrating rope supports over his head and hooked one rope with his left elbow. Orlo hollered as he slid closer to oblivion.

"Jon! Jon!" he screamed. "Hey, *Jon!*" Just as the stone started its drop over the edge, Jon snatched it up with his right hand. He flung Orlo as hard as possible to the forward bank. Then he dangled over the rope by his left elbow as if he were a wet towel.

The bridge reached the end of its arc and started to swing back. Its boards bobbed. The sound of cracking and splitting rope drew Jon's attention. Alarmed he reached out to the nearest rope support to stop his slide across the bridge bottom. He squeezed so hard his knuckles turned white from the effort. His feet clawed for traction until the rubber on the soles of his shoes hit solid board. No time to relax for, at that moment, the bridge let out a mighty and sharp crack as it reached the end of its second arc. The noise echoed throughout the chamber.

When the bridge reversed direction to swing back, Jon's body continued the swing and pivoted from the bottom out into space. Air rushed up from below and hit his back. His hands still gripped the rope support. It held. With great effort he pulled himself back between the side supports.

The bridge, a wild stallion trying to dismount an annoying rider, whipped back. Jon held tight then looked in horror as the supports groaned from strain behind him. The last twisted clump stretched out to its maximum and the thinnest rope pieces snapped one after another. He wouldn't make it to the shore!

He scrambled the next quarter of the remaining half but the end stayed out–of–reach. The rope let go; and Jon and the bridge started their fall together.

In the meantime, Orlo jumped into action on the bank. With cheeks billowed as large as basketballs, he blew a big strong wind out of his mouth and directed it under the falling bridge. The mini gale momentarily prevented the bridge end from descending toward the water—adding a couple brief minutes for Jon to finish his dash across the bridge and onto the safety of the hard ground. Behind him a long section of the bridge plunged into the water and splashed spray up on the steep rock walls. The wood disappeared under the foam and dissolved.

"That was rather a close one." Orlo commented as Jon crawled further up the path away from the fumes. Jon plunked himself on soft green moss where the path split in several directions.

"If this place gets worse the farther we go, I'm not sure I want to go further," he panted catching his breath.

Orlo comforted him. "You can eat and rest soon Jon. This path leads to Jarliss's chamber."

Jon crossed his arms and pursed his lips in a moment of defiance as Orlo steam-pointed to the right. However, his rumbling stomach welcomed the idea of food. His feet reminded him they wanted rest too. And meeting this Jharliss might prove interesting although Jon wasn't sure if one stone alone hadn't given him enough trouble.

He turned his attention back to the river. "What makes the river act that way Orlo?" Now safe and settled, his curiosity had kicked back in.

"It is the emotions of men. I'll inform you now so what you observe in the next chamber will not shock you." He hesitated and then continued, "The River is as one at the place we are approaching. It is neutral. Do you remember what I said concerning this land?"

"It is the land between the physical and the nonphysical."

"Yes, and souls of humankind pass through here on their journey to the Inner World. The special water of this river from the Inner World cleans the emotional energies gained in the Outer World so the souls can move on in a pure and neutral state. Otherwise, they would not be strong enough to bear the powers in their new dimension. The souls review their lifetime deeds once they are neutral and have passed on. This river then branches and flows to the Inner World. The refuse of negative emotions is carried in the water of one branch and positive emotions in the other. The bridges cross that double section here."

"Why don't they build the bridge over the neutral part?" Jon wondered aloud recalling his close escape. Wouldn't it hold up better there than it did here over the dark river?

"We must give the souls their space and Jon, you must not be worried in the next chamber. They will not bother us and it is forbidden for us to disturb them. Now we must hurry. Jharliss resides to the east. You can rest there. Proceed through this tunnel."

TEMPLE PRINCE

Four

The Chamber of Souls

Jon shuffled forward with sore legs and tired feet as he peered through the cone of light urging him closer to the next chamber's opening. Orlo, once again, clung to his shoulder. Jon's stomach screamed for food. How long he had been here?

My parents must be worried. I've been gone for so long.

He regretted having no way to send word he was okay. He even missed Andy, thinking how nice her familiar face would look after this strangeness.

A rising crescendo of voices funneled at him from the chamber. He peeked at Orlo whose eyes stared ahead half–lidded.

I guess it's OK to keep going.

A cacophony of a great multitude of people wailing, talking, shouting, and laughing escalated as he approached the bright opening of the tunnel's end. Though it, the curving ribbon of path continued atop a ridge high in the chamber. The wall fell away from the path in a steep vertical drop leaving a narrow ledge on which to walk.

"What is that...?" he directed to Orlo as he stepped out onto the ridge.

His words halted as a loud blended roar rushed at him from the cavern and hit him full blast. He gasped. A magnificent and terrible spectacle stretched across the wide river way below and filled the bottom of the cavern. Jon's throat tightened. He attempted a few more cautious steps onto the ridge before he stopped again, mouth hanging open. Orlo had not prepared him for this sight! Jon reached back to the rock wall along his left side for stability and took in the panorama.

Deafening noise filled a cavern larger than the first one he had entered which housed the two branches of the River of Deeds. A single river flowed across the subterranean floor, possibly as wide as a mile; the opposite side barely visible through filmy mists. Thousands of people floated through the water and merged into and out of foggy sections dotting the river.

They're not solid!

Orlo whispered, "The newly deceased."

These vaporous apparitions appeared in the same form they held at their deaths. Several individuals had lost limbs or showed evidence of disease. A foreign military man cradled his own decapitated head. Ghostly bodies of various ages swarmed in the waters. Newborn babies that recently passed away from life floated along on ethereal boats shrouded by mist. An eerie transparency blended them into the air at their edges. Many of the beings emitted a brilliant glow like Orlo's. Snippets of different languages wafted up to Jon's ledge.

Some of the spooky beings flitted around in confusion. Others proceeded ahead with serene faces and traveled through the water as if purpose guided them. Jon recognized no one. But several called out to each other.

Unbelievable!

The river remained as one wide channel where it hosted the specters. It continued downstream for a short way past the horde. At that point, it split into two distinct tributaries, each entering a separate tunnel running toward the chamber Jon had recently left. At the split, the water in each branch changed. The closest branch began to bubble and hiss. Its action accelerated into a frothy tumult as it reached the entrance to a low tunnel. The water in the farthest branch smoothed into moving silk before disappearing into another tunnel.

Jon looked back at the multitude. An order emerged amid the confusion. The spirits' greatest agitation occurred at the farthest reaches of the distant shore where they appeared out of nowhere in the mists near the bank. A third of them wailed in disorientation. Another third flitted around in every direction. The rest proceeded straight ahead and through the water in a quiet manner. The water rose to their waists. As they approached the middle of the river, most of them regained their composure. They looked around and caught sight of their surrounding companions. Here the noise swelled. Then gathering in one large mass, they progressed at an even pace across the river and toward, *him!*

He opened his mouth to scream, but the sound died in his throat. The ghoulish spirits grouped into an even regiment on his side of the river. The front lines turned in unison and floated straight toward him like an attacking army.

His shaking started again. His arms dripped sweat. With nowhere to run except back, he shrank into the adjoining rock and prepared for the worst. Teeth clenched and eyes closed, he braced himself for impact. Was there a defense against ghosts? He hadn't thought to ask Orlo. He closed his eyes and trembled.

Jon waited for the assault. Nothing happened! After a few moments he opened his eyes. Row after row of the regiment of placid spirits wafted into the flat vertical sparkling wall of rock that fell away below his feet. They ignored him as he hovered over them on the ledge! He relaxed and his lower jaw dropped again in wonder.

"Are you attempting to catch Musca domestica Linnaeus for your sustenance?" Orlo's mouth curled at the edges.

Jon suddenly felt foolish. He clamped his mouth shut. His eyebrows shot up as he turned toward Orlo.

Orlo muttered, barely audible, "Housefly. For dinner."

Orlo seared him with a stern look. It reminded Jon of his third grade teacher, Mrs. Wilson, who held the terror record of all time for his grade school. She must have been about a hundred years old and could flash freeze an entire auditorium with one vicious look.

Jon pulled himself together. Like a chipmunk crossing a busy highway, he scurried over the curving ridge, and he didn't dare glance downward. He flew into the next tunnel's entrance.

As Jon moved forward, eager to place the earlier experience behind him, he spotted motion in the passageway ahead. The ferret! This time Jon experienced no fear. The little ferret ran ahead and stopped before a smooth wall of stone. Part of the wall dissolved, and the ferret ran right through it. In seconds, the wall returned to normal.

Jon approached the same place. Orlo said, "Stand here a moment lad."

Unbelievable! The solid rock wall thinned and faded away in front of him.

Inside, a fire flickered in a small alcove near the back of a cozy chamber. An elegant woman stood in front of it next to a table displaying a row of lighted and partially melted candles, her back toward Jon. She stretched her arms out above the short flames and chanted a strange musical language in haunting tones. The melody reminded Jon of the music he heard near the first bridge. It stirred strange sensations in his chest.

The ferret lay in a fuzzy ball on a narrow ledge beside her, its eyes closed. Jon scanned the room for Orlo's twin stone, but found nothing.

The woman turned around to face him. Light streamed from her unlined face and caressed the rock walls of the cool room.

"Orlo, you have finally arrived!" Her voice stroked Jon's ears with soft lilting whispers that resonated through his body. "Come in, Jon, come in. Welcome to the Heart of the World. You are a brave lad coming here. This surely must be strange to you. I am Jharliss."

She smiled and bowed with the fluid grace of a ballet dancer.

"Nice to meet you, Ma'am."

He stared directly into her brilliant eyes. They transfixed him and sent tingles up and around his body that made him light–headed. Simultaneously, a scrunching happened inside his chest and time stopped. His mind floated into the air with impressions coming at him from every direction. He heard everything in the world in his head at once. If he picked out one stream he recognized where it originated and understood what they were thinking and feeling.

And, in one moment, he *connected* with her. He understood that she absorbed everything from him— his thoughts, his feelings, his memories, and maybe his future. She knew him better than he knew himself. She assimilated the worst in him and the best in him, everything he had done in his short life, including punching Andrea. It didn't matter to her. She completely accepted him. And *pure LOVE streamed* from her smiling eyes. His eyes watered as happiness lit up his spirit. He trusted her with his greatest secrets and fears.

"You are hungry and tired so we can talk later after you have had time to rest." Her expansive smile warmed him from the crown of his head to his toenails. "Then I'll answer your questions."

She motioned Jon to sit on a cushioned chair at a low stone table. Awe caused him almost to fall on the floor when he tried to sit. On the table lay a golden spoon beside a heavy bowl made of crystalline material. Hot cereal topped with large bumpy bright blue berries spilled over the top. Jon tasted the cereal and found it sweet. He gobbled every bit Stasos style.

Orlo dropped from Jon's shoulder and hopped across the hard floor making a clunking sound as he bounced. He planted himself near Jharliss' tiny feet. They resumed the chant together. Orlo's gruff voice created a baseline harmony resembling a Tibetan monk.

This gave Jon the opportunity to study Jharliss. A silver blue tunic skimmed over a lithe body to cover the top half of narrow pants. She stood not much taller than his 5'6" height. A wide band of sparkling flecks arranged in a spiral pattern adorned the tunic's hem. Short boots topped with light gray fur finished the outfit. The sparkling stones studding her boot tips made her feet flash as she moved in the soft glowing light of the candles.

Red hair streaked with gold hung to her waist. It twinkled from the shiny faceted ties that held several sections of her long hair pulled together and back from her face in loose waves. A soft glow encircled her body. Although she appeared youthful, Jon sensed that she was very old, ancient. An air of authority and great power mixed with compassion permeated her being.

Jharliss finished her musical chant and motioned him to a low rock ledge.

"Lie here for a while. It's not as hard as it looks. It will mold to your body when you lie upon it."

This idea agreed with Jon whose eyes, by this time, resisted staying open.

"Thank you Jharliss," he mumbled before he fell into a deep dreamless sleep on the odd but comfortable rocky bed.

Five

The Last Battle

Jon woke up hours later.

What's happening?

Across the room Orlo, Jharliss, and the ferret sat close together on three low rocks. They did not speak aloud. Their words appeared in his mind. He heard "training needs to start" and "is becoming acclimated faster than expected" and understood they talked about him. The ferret squeaked once in a while. She squeaked again and Jharliss turned to face Jon.

"You're rested and feeling better Jon. Good. We need to talk. A problem is developing in our world that affects your world. We think you can help," she said aloud.

Jon guessed his presence here was not an accident. These three were up to something that involved this Kaz person.

What could they want from me?

"Here is something for your nourishment." Jharliss offered him thick slices of sweet bread covered with a thin layer of honey and a chalice containing a delicious fruity drink. He savored the taste of these exquisite treats while Jharliss spoke in her melodic voice.

"We apologize for taking you away from your home and family. But quick action is required and you can help. Please consider what we have to show you."

Jharliss moved to a flat facet of the chamber wall and waved her hand once across its face. The rocky wall dissolved in the same way as the entrance to the chamber had dissolved earlier. Within it, a 3D image formed, a vision that portrayed a view of his house.

But what had happened?

The house stood vacant, and the roof had caved in on one side.

A large green tent was pitched in the yard behind the house. Next to it, Jon's father sat on a lawn chair talking to four strange men. Jon recognized one of them—Professor Gossmeyer, a naturalist at the University where his father taught. Jules talked as he looked across the clearing and toward the woods. He waited for someone.

"Me!" Jon exclaimed. "He is waiting for me, isn't he Jharliss? I've got to go home right now!"

"But where's Andrea? Where is my mother?" His forehead wrinkled into deep furrows.

"They are fine." Jharliss' voice was soothing. "They are staying with your Aunt Kate. They are safe although Andrea suffered a broken leg when a bureau toppled over on her. Don't worry, she is fine now."

Jon pushed himself away from the table. "I'm sorry," he said. "I need to go at once."

"Wait, Jon. There is more."

She passed her hand across the rock again. Orlo coughed from the same ledge where the ferret lay with both eyes glued on Jon. The scene within the rock changed to— Africa? A black man lay writhing on the ground. He coughed up blood. Another tough man stood over him with a rifle butt raised and ready to deliver another blow. The bruised and battered man lost consciousness—so terrible for Jon to watch, worse than the evening news.

The scene changed in a flash to South America. Guerillas in military fatigues fired mortars upon a small village. Helicopters fired rockets at buildings setting them on fire and blasting them to dust.

Men, women, and children, were running, crying, and screaming in confusion. Fire burned everywhere.

The scene morphed again. Middle Eastern men tossed hand grenades into a bus filled with people. The bus exploded with a loud blast and a huge cloud of smoke followed by more fire.

Jon turned his head. He couldn't watch more.

"What do these terrible things have to do with me, or my family, or those quakes? Or Kaz?"

"They are the result of the influence of a beast that will soon break free from our world to wreak destruction on your Outer World. It will destroy humankind, first mentally, and then physically. Great suffering, as never recorded in written human history, will follow. The devastation occurred one time, eons ago, but never with nuclear armaments or new kinds of germ warfare. Your world will change forever. Kaz attracts distorted minds into his energy field. The quakes you have been experiencing and the terror in the world mark the starting point of its influence."

"Who or what is Kaz, this beast?"

Orlo answered, "Kaz is a primordial evil created in this world, an instrument for balance from the Dark Powers. The polluted waters of the negative branch of the River of Deeds, from which he drinks, have created a hungry shadow in his spirit. Now a black stone lives in his heart and black goo fills his veins. We have contained him for eons but the potion we gave him is weakening. He will awaken soon. Resting in long hibernation has increased his power."

"In ages past, Kaz roamed throughout the world creating hysteria. You may have heard the ancient tales of dragons that scorched villages and stole gold and jewels. Most of those tales revolved around Kaz. And they are not just stories, but are true ancient history before men captured events in writing. Kaz is too sophisticated for that behavior now. His increased mental strength can force its way into the minds of people who are not strong enough to resist it."

"Realize that an idea precedes the action. People don't strive hard enough to hold a positive outlook during life's trials, so they are more likely to react with negative emotion like fear. Kaz's influence will end their chance to create happy and productive lives."

"People won't stand for it. Our government would bomb him."

Jharliss said, "That may be true—if they could detect his presence. He retains the ability to stay invisible by staying a half dimension away from you. He is too cunning to show himself. True evil hides. It gains power from its ability to work undetected."

"Why didn't you poison him and be rid of him forever?" Jon asked.

"Because we are Guardians, not destroyers. We care for everything in this land, including Kaz. Our rules for living are different here," Orlo explained.

"But how can *I* help? I'm only a boy."

"Yes, but a *physical* boy." Jharliss replied. "You're large enough to get through the grygots, which the Keepers find difficult due to their smaller size. Your body is small enough to maneuver through the tunnels to reach Kaz. And you run very fast when you try."

Orlo continued. "We could have handled Kaz alone, as in ages past, but Jharliss cannot leave this chamber anymore. What you see of her now is a strong energetic presence. This special chamber keeps her from passing to the Inner World. Kaz eliminated the physical in the last battle. I must remain as I am now too, until I pass. My stone figure, a gift from our friend Kaz a long time ago, has proved a useful disguise. It allowed me to pass into the Outer World but limits me now."

Jon stared at Jharliss. Was she a ghost? She didn't look vapory. Besides that, he had touched her solid arm.

Orlo went on, "Jharliss and I must continue to maintain balance in this land as long as we can. This helps to ease the souls' transitions between the Inner and Outer worlds. Soon a new millennium will start and new guardians will come to relieve us of our duty. Our primary and most urgent task is to contain Kaz so he cannot escape and annihilate the Outer world."

Jon remained silent for a moment. "I don't know what to do. I need time to think."

"As you wish, Jon," Jharliss responded. "We will leave you alone with your thoughts. Please think with your heart and not your head. And know this—everything is interconnected. What happens in your world affects our world, and what happens in our world affects your world."

She half turned then paused. "We will show you one more thing." Orlo added, "The Last Battle."

He blew steam at the rock facet. The flat rock dissolved, and the steam swirled through it then outside of it. Light and dark spots formed into a 3D shape and shot into the center of the room. Jon moved back.

The shape grew to twelve feet tall and details within smaller shapes emerged. A glow spread from the outer edges and increased in intensity until it lit up the room. A head formed at the top and Orlo's face emerged. His features appeared distinct, stronger than the vague impressions echoed by the rock which lay on the stone seat.

Orlo's body followed, composed from bits and pieces of smoky swirls. Soon an imposing figure stood in the center of the room facing Jon. Brilliant, wise, deep, eyes of piercing violet stared out from under high eyebrows on an elongated pale face. Shining silver hair curled around this face and fell below his shoulders. The long thin beard of a Chinese elder ended with a slight curl upon his chest.

This Orlo wore a silver tunic that stopped short of his knees. The front panel bore a woven symbol of two crossed ovals within a circle containing a central glowing star. The tunic fell over violet pants that tucked into smooth black boots.

Tall Orlo raised his right hand causing the entire room to swirl around Jon's head. Jon gripped his seat. Another image of Jharliss appeared. The two stood facing the edge of a vast sea with their backs to the smoldering ruins of a medieval city on Earth.

Something boiled beneath the surface of the troubled sea. Birds and nearby animals took flight in panic. A dark island crested the surface and rose from the water. The island turned into the top of a terrible head with batwing ears. When two yellow eyes with slit pupils emerged, the water itself tried to flow away. The full figure broke from beneath the water in one great movement to reveal a monstrous and terrifying dragon. Water streamed from its head and shoulders. The dragon smiled at the two adversaries standing on the shore, flicked up its tail, and roared.

Orlo lifted both hands summoning bolts of lightning from the sky to crash on the dragon's head. Kaz whirled and shot red–hot flames at the advancing lightning. To Jon's surprise, the powerful flames of Kaz pushed it back.

Jharliss spun her body to create a brilliant lariat of light. She swung it toward the dragon's neck. But before it released, Kaz confronted her with tremendous speed. He pulled his head back to scorch her with a missile of flames. Orlo ran between them, his flat hands stretched up with palms out, as a shield of light. The dragon fired an endless torrent against Orlo's shield. It incinerated every plant and tree around and melted portions of the sand into glassy chunks.

As it gained in width and strength, Orlo's eyes watered. He held strong with tremendous effort. Two slower crows above his head caught heat and burst into flames. They plummeted toward Orlo's feet causing a split second of distraction as he moved his feet back in reflex. This brief lapse changed Orlo and Jharliss forever. It allowed the shield to slip a mere half–inch to the left. The flames found their weak spot and streamed around the shield's edge to hit Orlo directly in his chest. He cried out.

To Jon's horror flames engulfed the magnificent guardian. He shrunk smaller and smaller, then lay as a chunk of burnt cinder on the sand.

In the meantime, Jharliss vaulted over Orlo's shrinking body. Her lariat flew to encircle Kaz around the neck and limit his movements. A hidden regiment of Keepers appeared from behind nearby scattered boulders and shot strong tranquilizer darts and arrows into the dragon. Kaz would sleep until Jharliss and Orlo discovered a more permanent method of containment.

The dragon's eyes glazed. His slow movements permitted one last blast at Jharliss. Caught defenseless, her body collapsed into a large globe of light. A bright spark glowed in the center.

The vision ended. Jharliss stepped forward and said, "The Keepers brought us back here, to our special chamber. It took a thousand years for our prime essence to replenish to the state we hold now."

"What happened to Kaz?"

"The Keepers arranged its movement back to one of the lower caverns with the aid of a resourceful friend. You may meet her later after your decision."

Jharliss picked up Orlo, and the two moved through another flat facet of the wall into a different room in the chamber to leave Jon alone to think. Before they left, Orlo reminded Jon, "Time is running out."

Jon lay back on the rocky bed. The ferret hopped up and settled in by his side. He wanted to help, but he didn't want to get involved. He wished this were an unpleasant dream from which he could awaken.

The vision with Kaz worried him greatly. This monster felt nothing for anyone or anything. And what had Jharliss said? It would never be seen so people wouldn't know of its existence.

Stroking the short white fur on the ferret's head his thoughts turned to home. He remembered the terror in his mother's eyes during the quakes. *And poor little Andy. She is so active. She must be miserable with a broken leg.* Jon regretted the way he had teased her. He vowed to be nicer to her if he ever got home.

Jharliss was right though. Harmful things happened in the world. The news was full of one terrible thing after another. Meanness and anger came naturally to unhappy people. It was part of being human wasn't it? He thought of himself. He didn't have to be nasty to Andrea. But she was such a baby, such a spoiled stinky little baby— always bugging him, always getting his parents to yell at him. Did they ever believe him? No! He decided to cream that little brat when he got home.

The ferret squealed breaking Jon's thoughts. A light current licked at his fingers and toes.

Why, another tremor! What was I thinking? Mean thoughts. Mean thoughts that aren't mine.

As a strange energy pervaded the air he sat up with immediate comprehension of the Guardians' dilemma. The twisted power of Kaz affected his thoughts and turned him against someone he loved. It amplified his small jealousies. How would it color his feelings toward strangers in the world? What if this happened to everyone? Was this the warning Jharliss tried to impress upon him?

Jon decided at that moment to accept their challenge and help Orlo and Jharliss fight this thing even though he wasn't sure how to help them.

"Thank you, Jon."

Jharliss appeared out of nowhere to stand at his side and Jon felt her presence before he saw her.

"You are wise to be fearful," she added. "Kaz could know you are coming and he might try to trick you. Keep your mind on your purpose and act with speed."

"Okay Jharliss. What do you want me to do?"

"First you must practice a few things. After that, we will show you our plan."

Ferret looked at her and disappeared into the other room. She came back holding a slingshot between her tiny jaws.

"Have you ever used one of these?" Jharliss asked.

Orlo interrupted and chortled from the table, "Oh, ho ho. David and Goliath. Oh ho ho." He laughed so hard he wobbled.

Jon snatched the slingshot and whizzed a nearby pebble right past Orlo's ear. He was good at skipping stones and better at hitting a target with a slingshot. His father had made him one to chase rabbits away from his mother's garden.

Jon replied in his most casual tone, "Oh once or twice," and tossed Orlo a small smile.

"You must be fast and your aim sure," Jharliss cautioned as she laid several stones of various sizes on the table near Orlo.

Jon picked up one small stone and Orlo tested him blowing a steam ring up into the air.

"Hit that!" he challenged and Jon let the shiny pebble fly for a near miss.

"Oh ho ho. It must have been once," Orlo teased. He blew another ring up and this time Jon's stone sailed through it.

"Faster," Orlo urged and blew two rings into the air.

Jon hit the first dead center, missed the second.

"Faster," Orlo repeated as he puffed out three rings.

Jon concentrated and whipped three stones into the sling, one after another. The first passed through the center of Orlo's steam ring. The second nudged the outside of its ring. And the third yelled, "Yahhhhhhhhhhh," as it sailed through the center of the third steam ring.

Jharliss laughed, and the ferret leaped to catch a screaming Orlo as he zoomed toward the floor.

Jon dipped his head. "Sorry Orlo."

The stone huffed back, "Well, good aim boy. This plan may truly succeed."

Six

Magda and Amara

The next day Jharliss dazzled Jon with a full smile as she called out, "Good morning, Jon. It's time to wake up."

She sat on a small boulder with a flat top and a slight depression that hugged her bottom. She motioned Jon to sit by her side.

"I'm sending you to a special chamber to meet an old friend of mine. Her name is Magda. Magda is our expert on every plant on the earth and other places. We need a drug potent enough to put Kaz back to sleep for a long time and we can only get this from Magda. However, she will require a trade. The sprites never give goods away for free. They believe you won't appreciate a thing that isn't worked for or paid for." She paused and wrinkled her forehead. "We must disguise you. They won't let you into the garden if they know you are human and they certainly won't trade with you."

She walked to a flat vertical rock near the back of her small chamber room. When she placed her hand against the rock face, it dissolved. Shelves filled with various bowls of powders and dried fruits—a pharmacy of sorts—appeared behind it.

Jharliss selected three little blue berries.

"Here, eat these, Jon. Don't be afraid. They will reduce your size. A race of Keepers exist called Harpeni. They think with a group mind and are telepathic. Their reputation as peace negotiators is well known and, they travel often. They don't use names. They go by the name Harpeni to others. Occasionally they send out an ambassador to visit the various groups. Their anatomy is humanlike although they are much smaller. And, they are . . . *blue.*"

She winked. "Can you flutter your hands?" She moved the tips of her fingers higher and lower with quick short movements. "Harpeni flutter their hands when they get nervous so, if someone gets suspicious, do this." Jon practiced. It was easy enough, he thought.

"Rest for a while. As you rest, imagine yourself shrinking to the size of a mouse. When you awaken, you will find yourself smaller."

Jon followed her instructions. He pictured himself as a petite gray mouse. As the berries worked, he dozed off into a deep sleep.

When he woke up, his rocky bed had grown very large! To his surprise, he had been sleeping in the huge neck hole of a shirt! He walked to the edge of his bed and looked out over the room. It, too, had grown bigger.

Loud snoring came from a dim corner and he spotted Orlo, who had grown to the size of a boulder! Things looked different from what he remembered. He glanced at his hands and his now naked body. His breath stopped short. He was blue! His pale skin had taken on the pale blue cast of a person needing a lot of oxygen. And he had shrunk! His body had morphed into a tiny size, one that made a small mouse look large. What a strange feeling! He wasn't sure he liked this.

Orlo stirred and grunted. "Good morning, Harpeni. I must say Jon, that color compliments you."

The ferret, now huge, jumped up beside Jon and almost knocked him off his bed ledge. Its teeth held tiny blue pants with a thin rope belt and a short sleeved shirt in a darker shade of Jon's skin. Jon dressed in rush so Jharliss wouldn't find him naked.

"Climb up on the ferret's back. Hold on to her fur and she'll give you a ride to the Garden," Orlo suggested.

Jon grabbed the ferret's neck fur and pulled himself over the top of her back. He swung his legs around and straddled the ferret's neck above her shoulders and right behind her ears.

She makes a nice soft mount, he thought as he adjusted his grip on her short white fur.

The ferret landed on the floor with a fluid motion, much smoother than any horse he had ridden. *How fun!* Maybe his small size wasn't so bad!

Jharliss entered the room. Jon gripped the ferret with his knees and fluttered his hands. She laughed.

"Being small is different, isn't it? Don't worry. It won't be long until you are comfortable with it and your mount. Now, I'll give you something Magda will prize."

She handed Jon a couple tiny brown seeds wrapped in a dried but pliant leaf. Black dots peppered their surface.

"I'll put these in a small pouch. Tie them to your belt now, and then offer to trade them for Amara when you meet her. Waste no time. We must hurry."

Orlo called out to them as the ferret shot through the doorway. "And don't get involved with those fairies. Use your wiser self."

Little blue Jon, the new Harpeni, gripped the neck fur as the ferret sped through various tunnels for hours. The tight tunnels had just enough room to allow passage for the ferret and rider. As they rode through the wider tunnels the ferret bucked like a bronco to thrill Jon.

Whoopee!

At last she entered a series of grassy tunnels and waited before a flat wall of shiny moss.

"Who desires to enter?" A young male voice called out from the wall.

The ferret squeaked and a young man's face appeared from behind the moss.

"Ferret? From Jharliss? Of course. Welcome."

The wall dissolved and, the ferret bounded through the entry to stop before a young green man a bit larger than Jon. A pointy little nose and ears stuck out of his face. His bright blue eyes glowed. He wore a flexible leaf tunic in green tied at the waist with a cord made of multiple twisted plant fibers.

"I say there, Harpeni?" he asked looking at Jon.

"Yes, what's your name?" Jon asked trying to be friendly.

"Name? We don't name ourselves. I'm a sprite."

He looked at Jon with suspicion and sniffed.

"Are you sure you're not hu—man? You smell hu—man."

Jon fluttered his hands as Jharliss had taught him.

A girlish voice came from above Jon's head.

"He's cute. Harpeni of course."

"Yes Harpeni," echoed from two different high—pitched voices.

Jon spotted three bright lights fluttering toward him through the trees. A glowing golden girl sporting four short ponytails and four translucent dragonfly wings flitted close and slid right behind Jon on the ferret's back.

"I'm Hesperia."

She hugged his waist. Jon caught a whiff of a delicate and familiar perfume, Lily of the Valley!

"You don't have a name." The sprite crossed his arms with a disgusted look on his face.

"Yes, and I'm Hypatia," laughed the second glowing girl with pink hair and pink translucent wings as she slid behind Hesperia, giggling.

"Oh, well yes. And I'm Helena," said the third as she swooped in front of the ferret's nose.

She ruffled Jon's hair as she passed him.

What a cute giggle. Jon smiled at her. She bore the same greenish cast as the sprite. She winked with a large green eyes and long dark eyelashes and smiled back at him.

The young sprite rolled his eyes.

"Leave those fairies alone, if you know what's good for you, Harpeni," he warned as he pushed Helena away and took hold of the ferret's left ear.

He pushed both Hypatia and Hesperia from the ferret's back.

"They're nothing but trouble."

The fairies flitted around in the air behind Jon and the ferret talking among themselves.

The sprite took charge. "Welcome, then. What is your business here, Harpeni?"

"Jharliss sent me . . . to Magda."

"The old crone? She's not taking audience right now."

"Oh, but I must visit her. I've been instructed to give her these." He showed the seeds to the sprite.

"Those aren't," he stammered. "Aren't they... oh, my"... he looked at them again. "Oh my... Well, maybe she *will* meet you."

Jon slid the precious seeds back into his pouch. His eyes circled the remarkable chamber. A thick jungle of plants rose around him to create a tropical paradise of colors and smells. The dense leaves blocked most of his view to a golden sky that hung overhead. *Was the sky artificially made? Or natural to this area?*

The sprite warmed up at Jon's wide-eyed look of appreciation.

"Nice place," Jon mused.

"Only place this complete in the entire universe. We cultivate at least one of each."

"Each?" Jon queried.

"Each plant from the Outer World."

Clearly the sprite took pride in this accomplishment.

"This is the Botanical Library. A good many of these plants are extinct now in the Outer World. You know those hu–mans are such ignorant creatures. They don't value their gifts and they don't cooperate with other species. They can't even get along with their own." He stated the last with disgust.

"Yes, you're right." Jon agreed with a slight flush of shame.

"And it's a good thing you aren't hu–man Harpeni, because, Magda would eat your head for dinner. Hu–man brains, her favorite." He grinned.

Jon felt queasy and checked his hands to make sure his blue color held. *Yes, still blue.* He sighed with relief.

"Just be careful of the insects." The sprite continued as he made his way through the forest of plants. "They're not very smart. They don't mean to harm anyone but sometimes they're just clumsy. We need them around to help protect the plants. We even keep a wolf spider or two. Want to see one?"

Jon knew he should hurry to Magda but, he didn't want to offend his host.

"Sure!"

The sprite chatted away merrily and ushered Jon and the ferret to the rim of a gorge where a team of sprites pushed a bound aphid over the edge.

"A scourge for the plants," the sprite explained as the group grunted and groaned under the weight.

The aphid tumbled a good distance to the bottom. Jon looked with horror at the huge hairy spider with gaping jaws that stood waiting for his treat. The spider responded to the sprites hand signal like a well–trained dog. *It might do tricks for more aphids.*

"We keep it fed, so it doesn't bother us much. It is all in a spirit of cooperation. Our first responsibility is to the plants."

Jon fluttered his hands.

The sprite laughed, "Oh, don't worry. He won't bother you. Just his brothers and sisters!"

"I'll take you to the edge of Magda's woods. You'll have to go on alone from there. I'll meet you again when you come out. *If* you come out," he added.

The sprite led Jon to a path framed by a magnificent floral archway of rhododendron. It wound through a forest of plant stems. John recognized plants from his mother's garden.

"Well, this is as far as *I* go," the friendly sprite said as he stopped. "Magda does not take kindly to uninvited guests."

He said goodbye. Jon was left to travel the path with the ferret. The further they went, the more she slowed and dragged her feet.

Ahead in a small clearing, stood an odd little house fashioned from a generous sized coconut. An elaborate carved door hung on the front, its intricate designs out of place with the rest of the modest home.

"All right, wait here." Jon slid off his skittish mount.

An animal skull loomed on a tall post outside the doorway as a sentry. Jon stared at hollow orbs that had once held eyes. Pointy teeth, still intact in the long jaws, jutted toward him. *Grygot?* Now his feet dragged as he inched toward the entrance of the odd house.

He just approached the door when a brusque voice shot out.

"Halt!"

He halted.

"Who dares to come here? Have you not heard I am not receiving visitors right now?"

"It is just I, Harpeni," answered Jon in a small voice.

At once the superb door flew open. The doorway filled with a mass of woman. She had no visible neck. Double chins rested on her chest. Orange hair stuck out from her head in tight springs and her eyes squinted at him under bushy eyebrows. Her skin color matched the sprite's green. A thready brown tunic and pants hung saclike on her body. Small animal teeth formed the decorative pattern sewn on her tunic's hem. Another set of teeth created a double stranded necklace around her neck.

"What is your business?" she demanded in a sharp voice. She rested her arm on a thick gnarled staff to prop up her enormous bulk.

"I come as a trader from Jharliss. She needs some Amara for Kaz."

"And what business is that of ours?" she snapped turning back.

"These are for you." Jon offered the seeds.

She swung around to check out the seeds then gasped, "Where did you get these?" She fingered the leaf gingerly and her hands trembled.

Then she caught herself and pierced Jon with an intense stare.

"You have a large head."

He fluttered his hands.

"Hmm, Harpeni. Smell like hu–man."

She crossed her arms and turned her head to one side. When she pivoted toward her door Jon thought she intended to leave him.

"Ok. You come in. I will give you Amara for the seeds of the Oracle plant. And," she paused, "only for those seeds."

Jon fluttered his hands to keep his attention focused on his task. He did not relish entering this strange woman's home. The skull leered at him as he passed.

A pungent odor assaulted Jon's nostrils when he stepped through the door. He checked out objects in the windowless house with the faint light that filtered through the door's cracked opening. A large rocking chair occupied one section. Across from it, a leaf–covered bed supported by a spongy material filled the other main space. It sagged at the center. Shelves full of ground substances, powders, twigs, and dried leaves lined four walls.

Magda shuffled over to a small gray pitcher and poured golden liquid into a small waterproof pouch. Reaching up to the top shelf, she pushed several jars out of the way to retrieve a bottle of gold powder from the back. She mixed this into the liquid and handed the bag to Jon with a grunt.

He presented the precious Oracle seeds in return.

"You will be a young man when this plant from the Inner World comes to maturity. It takes many years for it to mature. I will be an old woman. Now leave me Hu–man."

Jon flinched and saw in her eyes that she did not believe his story for a minute. She knew exactly who he was. He did not wait for a second invitation to leave. He raced out the door to the path where he found the ferret sleeping under a sheltering plant. The ferret awoke with a start when Jon leaped on her back. They sped toward the entry to Magda's woods.

The sprite was nowhere to be seen when they emerged, but his girlfriends Hesperia, Hypatia, and Helena fluttered around in alternating circles.

"What are you carrying, Harpeni?" they asked when they spotted the pouch.

"Oh, nothing really."

He tried to push the pouch into the waist of his trousers.

"Did you get that from Magda?"

Helena and Hypatia glided in like swallows and held Jon's hands back. Hesperia flipped by at the same time, kissed him on the ear, and snatched up the pouch. The ferret turned her head and snapped at the fairies with no result. The three fluttered into a circle overhead to open and inspect the contents.

"Ooh… A mara. Who do we need to put to sleep?" they giggled.

"Hey! Give that back," Jon demanded.

"We could use this. I know a couple irritating wolf spiders we could put out for a long time."

"That's not yours. You have no right…" but the fairies were not listening.

They flitted around in circles giggling and then flew off to another path with Jharliss' precious Amara. Jon had no choice but to urge the ferret to chase after them.

The ferret and rider bounced rapidly over a long path heading away from the entrance to the chamber to chase the fairies. The fairies flew in a wavelike motion, up and down, and stayed ahead of them. They played catch with the prized package and, every few minutes they glanced back to tease. Jon had gained on them when the five neared another clearing.

On their approach, the ferret stumbled on a fat root crossing the path. Jon tumbled into the center of the clearing head over heels. A haphazard stack of logs masquerading as giant sawn trees bordered the right side. Something moved near the top of the pile. When Jon stood up to get a better vantage the chewed leg of a wolf spider vaulted over the top of the pile and landed at his feet.

Less than a minute later, giant antennae covered with dense hairs rose from behind the wood followed by a set of enormous eyes. Next, three segments of a creature whose head sported huge pincers eased into view. Two legs waved from opposite sides of each segment. Six legs wriggled in different directions as the creature opened huge threatening jaws to confront Jon. With one leap it could be upon him. This called for fast action. He surveyed the clearing perimeter for something to use in defense.

The ferret recovered her footing, and she leapt over Jon's head to land halfway between him and the insect creature. She matched the creature's size. Not to be deterred, the creature set its six legs on the pile and lunged forward with amazing speed to reveal a horrendous plated and segmented body with *hundreds* of legs. The ferret dove to catch a third leg as the front of the creature reached the end of the wood pile and lifted to an arch. She and the creature flipped over together, leaving the creature on its side, legs writhing back and forth, and the ferret on her back.

In the meantime, the fairies had stopped flying away. They wanted to be chased and, now that Jon no longer pursued them, the fun had ended. They doubled back and gasped when they spied Jon and the ferret confronting the twitching segmented body.

"Chilopoda," they screamed in unison, "centipede."

Hypatia yelled, "Run away. It's poisonous!"

Hesperia swooped over the centipede with the pouch.

Helena flew in to help her and pointed to the head. "Over here. It will splash off the segments."

Together they pulled the pouch open and splattered a few drops over the creature's head. It dripped into the eyes and stung. The angry creature thrashed around, its hundred legs everywhere at once.

The centipede twisted its body around to set a third of its legs on the ground and popped its body upright. It whirled around in a fierce attack. Jon brandished a long pointy stick that he had picked up to help the ferret.

The centipede lowered the rest of its huge body and lunged. With pincers opening and closing it prepared for the kill. Then it fell into a wretched heap inches from Jon's feet. The Amara worked!

The sprite emerged from the forest path behind them. It didn't take him long to figure out the events of the past few moments.

"Give that back," he ordered the fairies. "He could have been killed. Fairies," he muttered under his breath. "Nothing but trouble. Really Harpeni, I told you to stay away from them."

The fairies showed no remorse as Hesperia dropped the pouch at Jon's feet. Chastised, they turned to fly away.

"We'll be back later," they promised. Their little mouths puckered and blew kisses to Jon before they zipped away into the trees one after another.

Only a few drops of Amara were missing, so Jon decided to continue his trip back to Jharliss. Besides, he had no more seeds to trade with Magda.

He and the sprite mounted the ferret together. The sprite guided him back to the entrance of the chamber.

TEMPLE PRINCE

Seven

Training

The next morning, Jon shed the grogginess of a heavy slumber and opened his eyes. To his relief he found himself back to his normal size.

He inspected the back of his hands. *Still blue, although lighter.*

Two more days passed before the blue pigment faded totally. During that time, the quakes continued. Jon barely heard their long low rumbling but, their vibrations crawled over his skin with an icky presence. Although they remained mild, a few lasted a long time. Each quake sent an ominous chill up his spine.

Mission training, with both Orlo and Jharliss, lasted two days. They made him practice with the slingshot until he could hit a moving target within an inch nine out of ten times.

When he took aim Orlo instructed, "Focus on the target alone. Forget everything else. Strengthen your will." The ferret assisted by retrieving the small stones and returning them to a small pile near his feet.

Orlo sent him racing through the adjacent tunnels with the ferret as a good running partner.

What an amazing creature! She is both helpful and friendly.

Jon and the ferret hurdled and dodged rocks until he flew like a sonar–guided bat. In one wild and crazy dash, the ferret jumped up, bounced off the top of a waist high rock, and landed on top of his head! Jon laughed as he reached up and rescued her.

Orlo cautioned, "Quick reactions and decisions are vital in this mission. You freeze when you are startled or frightened. Overcome and focus."

Jon discovered that lectures began during breaks. Orlo started out by clearing his throat, puffing out his cheeks, and pursing his lips.

"Hmm, Humph. The macrocosm is reflected in the microcosm."

"What?"

Orlo blew a spurt of steam to direct Jon's attention to the flat wall. Swirling designs in vivid hues of blue, purple, gold, and aqua spread out across the flat rock screen.

"Fractals. Patterns within patterns."

Jon looked hard at the design.

What was he supposed to see?

"Oh, I see it!"

He pointed out a small section that was the exact color and shape of a larger section.

"What does it mean?"

"Mysteries within mysteries," Orlo continued. "The whole is contained in the part."

"Oh, OK, I get it. You mean the small design carries the information of the entire picture. Right?"

Orlo didn't answer. He'd skip to the next idea. "Wholeness."

"What?"

"We are the wholeness. The world is inside us." Orlo's eyes glazed and he stared up at the ceiling at that point. "What is without, is within."

This last remark had something to do with Kaz and himself, but Jon wasn't getting it. Orlo talked in riddles.

The final and hardest part of Jon's training was a strange mind game conducted by Jharliss.

"This is your most important exercise," she cautioned." Now remember something that happened in your life and concentrate on that one thing."

He tried to picture his room at home—his toys, books, and his aquarium. Before he knew it, something else distracted him—a race or a game he had played with Andy or, worse yet, the grygots. Jharliss had replaced his image with one of her own.

Jharliss patiently reminded him, "Stay focused, Jon. Resist my thoughts."

After two partial days of practice, Jon discovered he could set up a mental wall to block out her will. He held the wall for several minutes to half an hour depending on how hard he concentrated.

"Form positive thoughts too, and stay in the present moment," she advised as she performed another task, mixing a medicine for a Keeper family.

This too, proved difficult at first. But Jon's practice paid off. He held those good thoughts longer and longer. His mind paid attention to the here and now and did not stray to what had happened in the past or what might happen in the future.

At last, Jharliss determined he was as prepared as time allowed.

"Close your eyes, Jon."

In a moment, she said, "Now open."

Four items lay side–by–side on the stone table beside Orlo. The first was a shield made of the same shining see–through material as the bowl from which he ate during his first meal with Jharliss. Three tiny globe–like vials encapsulated the Amara and lay beside the shield. Three chances to put Kaz back to sleep.

"Lift the shield," Jharliss instructed. He grasped an inside handle and punched the shield outward in several directions. He found it as light as aluminum.

"It won't help you much against Kaz. But it should be helpful in keeping the grygots sharp teeth away from your limbs. You will have to contend with them before you reach Kaz's chamber."

Jon's stomach churned at the mention of those grygots. He certainly did not want to meet them again. They were more frightening than the huge wolf spider. They reminded him of a pack of enraged pit bulls.

Jharliss' eyes went to the vials.

"Yes, Jon, these contain the sleeping potion. They should fit in your sling. You have only three chances so you can see why it is so important that your aim be accurate. You must aim at one of Kaz's body openings. His mouth will be the best place but not the easiest target. Several holes on his underside can absorb the potion. Even an ear or an eye will be acceptable although it will take longer there for the potion to be absorbed by his body. The vial should dissolve soon after impact. *And remember, the entire content of at least one vial must be entered into Kaz for full effect.*" She stressed this last part of her instructions.

Orlo broke into the conversation, "We have arranged for Reil to send a team to help you get past the grygots."

He puffed his cheeks out. "Of course, I will be there to assist you in any way possible. Ferret must return here in the event she is needed by Jharliss."

Jon nodded. He reached for the vials and fingered them.

As he slipped the bottles into his leather pouch, Jharliss opened a small sliding door that blended into the cave wall. A vegetable dish covered with an herb sauce and a luscious array of fruit sat on a small tray.

Jharliss handed him the tray, "Here is your last meal with us. For strength."

Jharliss placed a small bowl on the floor in front of the ferret. Then she turned to light three white candles. She chanted in low musical tones, in her strange language while Jon and the ferret finished their meals. At last, she turned around with face glowing. An enhanced halo of white light surrounded her body before fading out at the edges.

"I'll strap you onto Jon's belt Orlo. Sorry, but he must keep his hands free."

Orlo winced as she slid him into Jon's Native American leather pouch to sit like a sardine between the vials. She tugged the drawstring tight and offered the package to Jon.

"Thank you, young friend," she said as she gazed at Jon with serious eyes. "I have confidence in you. Have confidence in yourself. Remember, be of one mind. Focus. React with speed. We will meet again in the Inner World. Remember, let peace and love be your companions in all your journeys."

Orlo's muffled voice came from Jon's belt, "Follow ferret. She'll lead you to Reil and the others."

Jon's heart sank when he turned to leave Jharliss. She had been so kind and loving— as much as his mom. But now it was time to carry on with his dreaded task. He needed to get back to his family and show them how much he cared for them.

His eyes misted at the corners. "Goodbye Jharliss. I love you."

Then he turned to follow the ferret into the tunnel to meet the others.

An eerie and unusual silence settled over the team of sentry grygots waiting in a tunnel far below the River of Deeds. The air crackled with anticipation.

The tunnel ended at small gray wooden door. Something stirred beyond that forbidding door: a huge horrible mass, evil incarnate, twisted and ugly in mind, body, and spirit.

It lifted an eyelid over a slanted eye, then paused before both eyes opened wide. Yellow eyes narrowed in amusement as it appraised the status of the transitional world with intuitive understanding. Something insignificant was coming toward it. A boy! How fortunate! A *human* boy carrying a shield made by those old fools, the Guardians. The monster's thin lips curled into a derisive smile. It smacked its lips in anticipation of the scrumptious taste of boy, a replacement for those cooked human meals when he entered the Outer World—meals he would miss since he planned to stay hidden from the physical realm. The elixir produced by men's hate and anger due to his inspiration would offer ample satisfaction.

Until then, they were going to play a game. This warm–up exercise in terror would feed Kaz's lust for chaos, a small appetizer before it broke free into the Outer World for the real fun. It snorted with delight. The creature stretched and scratched its claws against the rock. Its eyes closed. Now to for the human as a spider waits for a fly. The gargantuan monster feigned sleep and waited.

The ferret guided Jon with precision through the Chamber of Souls. As they hurried across the high pathway, Jon observed the orderliness of the procession of spirits merely going on with their business. This time he felt no fear. They posed no threat.

Continuing on, the ferret, Orlo, and Jon entered the open spot of land where he had ended his crossing at the River of Deeds. A new wooden bridge swung over the rotten branch of the river. The unweathered golden brown of fresh hewn wood replaced its missing floorboards.

Reil stood waiting by the bridge, stretched to his full height, shoulders back, and head tipped up. Fifty of the Keepers accompanied him. They wore leather breastplate armor decorated with a stamped metal plate that bore an insignia of a star surrounded by two crossed ovals within an outer circle. A painted quiver filled with wooden tubes and short feathered darts hung from their backs. No armor protected their legs or arms.

I guess they travel light.

When he saw them armed and ready he thought: *This confrontation is going to happen. I'm going to meet a monster… Kaz.*

He pinched himself. *Yes, it's real.*

He hesitated and turned back toward the tunnel after having second thoughts on his participation. But not before Reil hailed, "Greetings Jon." Reil bowed, the corner of his mouth twitching.

"Greetings Reil." Jon returned the bow.

Too late to leave now. He reaffirmed his resolve to continue on and do his best with this mission.

Reil briefed Jon on their strategy. They would follow the tunnel that ran beside the low river to a branch that ended at Kaz's chamber. The sentries waited there, and the Keepers planned to protect Jon as he made his way to Kaz's chamber. They wanted to creep up and surprise the grygots. At that point, the Keepers would attack full force with their tranquilizer darts and divert the grygots' attention away from Jon.

He added, "You will be their biggest surprise. No human has ever left the transition chamber."

"Slip through the little door at your first opportunity. We'll watch your back. Just get to that monster nice and quiet, lad. Then let him have it. Don't wait around until the Amara takes hold. Get yourself out of there as fast as ya can. That potion will sting him and, for sure, he'll wake up. An' no matter how much training Jharliss gave ya, you're no match for the likes of Kaz."

"Keep Orlo with ya, too. Ya need to take good care of him for, if anything unexpected happens, he'll need to advise ya of what to do next. He'll show you the way out through the tunnel. Ya can cross the bridges now. We fixed them and they're safe. Orlo will direct ya back to the Outer World."

Reil reached into his quiver and pulled out a dart.

"These are tipped with a powerful sleep medicine," he said as he held up the dart's small and extremely sharp point. "They have worked well to stop grygots in times past."

He grinned.

Jon untied the drawstring to the leather pouch. He patted Orlo on the head like a pet kitten. Orlo grimaced.

"Here are the vials."

"They contain rare medicine indeed." Reil nodded his approval. "That will surely do the trick. We won't be seeing Kaz around here for a long time."

He nodded to Orlo.

The symbol on the tiny breastplate caught Jon's attention.

"What does it mean Reil?" His index finger lightly traced the strange insignia etched into the metal.

"It is symbolic of the soul in our world," Orlo answered for Reil. "The circle represents the universe. The two ovals stand for the Inner World and the Outer World. Our world is symbolized by the intersection of the two ovals. The star stands for the shining soul that travels in all three worlds."

Jon's pouch vibrated. Orlo began to hum a haunting melody.

"Set me out on the floor Jon. We must perform the Ritual of Success."

Jon gently settled Orlo on the stone floor within a semicircle of the Keepers. Light emanated from his face and illuminated the troop. They shifted around and adjusted their equipment with slight quiet movements. Orlo grew brighter. The volume of his humming rose then lowered in waves of sound. Jon studied its effect on Reil and the Keepers. Their pupils dilated and, they became still.

Orlo spoke now. His voice resonated within Jon's being.

"Choice becomes the future. We go forward into time through the present. Our hearts and minds are clear. We envision the fruit of success in our endeavors. We hold the brave deeds of our forefathers buried in our bones. They are our legacy of courage. Our hearts and our minds are clear. We act with strength in our intention. We do what is necessary to achieve our goal. Our hearts and minds are clear."

"We see the great sea of souls directed toward the greater good and know that we are one with that sea. The doorway to the Inner World arises in our allotted time when we become embraced by joy."

The keepers responded in unison, "Our hearts and minds are clear."

A young Keeper with red cheeks blasted out a few tinny notes on a small trumpet.

After a moment of silence, Reil announced with his jaw set hard, "The time has come."

Reil, Jon, and the others descended through the opening of a lower tunnel near the putrid branch of the River of Deeds.

TEMPLE PRINCE

Eight

Battle with the Grygots

Jon's nose itched.

What is that disgusting odor coming from the river?

A dark sticky curtain of discomfort dropped over him and pricked his back as the tunnel descended steeply. He leaned back to maintain his balance and steady his footing.

Reil and the other Keepers marched in front of him, brave knights holding their heads high.

Jon took courage from their impressive bravery. He knew they were outnumbered and way outsized by the grygots. Yet they marched forward without hesitation. Only a couple near the back of the group lagged and shifted uncomfortably.

The poor visibility increased with each step. The group quieted as oppressing blackness wound around their arms and legs. The air turned damp and a sharp coldness stabbed at their muscles and bones. Jon's muscles stiffened.

What's that?

Small movements near the tunnel floor revealed a nasty looking beetle–ish bug poking its head out from a jagged crack in the wall. As Jon watched it crawl, something landed on the back of his neck. He flinched at a prick and heard a familiar buzzing.

Mosquitoes! They swarmed into the tunnel by the hundreds.

Reil instantly produced a small pouch of ointment from a pocket on his quiver and rubbed its gel–like contents on his neck. "Try this," he said as he handed it to Jon.

Similar pouches appeared from the other Keepers and they vigorously rubbed the contents over their faces and necks. Jon had worn long pants and a shirt with long sleeves when he set out from home. Now he was grateful for the extra protection. The mosquitoes buzzed around them hungrily, but did not bother them again.

Jon's emotions shifted around as he penetrated deeper into the blackness. He had overcome his trepidation when they first descended and had forced himself to find the courage within to go ahead. Now, as his uneasiness increased, he grew more irritable. His head throbbed from pressure building at his temples.

An awareness of his large size next to the Keepers began to occupy his thoughts. He towered over the largest one, and he had to be very careful as his slightest bump could knock them completely off their feet.

They are so small.

Why, I am a giant compared to them!

An electric current zapped through his mind. He could be their KING. Power surged through his body making him feel strong and brave. None of these little guys had the ability to stop him if he demanded their attention and obedience.

Low throat clearing came from the leather pouch. The noise broke Jon's thoughts. His face reddened.

What am I thinking? Where did that idea come from?

He did not want to be king. He just wanted to get home.

Why, that dark energy is present again!

It pulled at his mind, dragging him to black and weighty thoughts. A low level vibration ran through his body.

He snapped his attention back to the mission. It required his highest resolve to keep his mind directed toward his purpose, so he *willed* himself strongly to stay focused.

An occasional pant or sigh sifted through the group. Reil raised a finger to his lips to signal quiet. A foggy stream drifted out of the leather pouch. The stream of fog spewed out faster and hugged their arms and legs.

Orlo created a blanket of fog to mask their positions as they approached the grygots. The grygots foul smell would give away their positions. The Keepers had to depend on stealth and their superior eyesight to hold the loathsome creatures at bay until Jon made his way through the door.

The low volume of a familiar clacking bounced at them from ahead. Tension knotted in his stomach.

Breathe deep, he told himself. He consciously relaxed his stomach muscles and pulled air into his lungs.

He stepped forward. Whack! A large barbed claw abandoned on the tunnel floor like an old dry bone skittered away from him and crashed into a large rock. The troop stopped at once and listened for change in the noise ahead. But the discordant noise of the clacking continued.

The troop crouched low in the fog as they neared a sharp bend in the tunnel. They waited for Reil's signal. Jon fingered the vials in his pouch and touched Orlo for reassurance. The quantity of Orlo's fog intensified, streaming out as thick clouds that filled the tunnel in front of them. Then Reil raised his tiny arm and the small band loaded darts into the hollow tubes. The troop raised their blow tubes to their mouths. Reil lowered his arm, and they surged forward in unison. With cheeks billowed out, the front line of Keepers burst around the curve into the snarling mass of grygots. Darts flew— phfft, phfft, phfft— and two black shapes fell with a crack.

The grygots reacted at once. The nearest group jumped back and pivoted around rapidly to scope out the extent of the threat. Their eyes darted back and forth across the front of the wall of fog. Two of them jumped forward with gnashing teeth but found no mark.

The mist effectively hid Reil's small troop. Jon watched the Keepers' quick shadows dash through thin patches of fog. Three grygots crashed to the floor.

With his shield held out, Jon advanced into a blur of grygots. A grygot scraped against it, bounced back, and swung around in full charge. Just behind it, two Keepers stepped out of the mist. They prodded at its hindquarters with tiny pointed spears. It ignored them and proceeded to provoke Jon. A dart whizzed by from over his head and wedged into the neck of the oncoming grygot. The creature dropped at Jon's feet. Jon glanced up at a ledge above and found the source of the darts, two Keepers who alternately fired into the swarm of grygots. Their good marksmanship and high position kept them out of danger.

Orlo shouted into his mind, "The door. Go forward. Find the door Jon."

Jon looked straight ahead. Nothing was there except fog. It only permitted him to see an arm's length around his body. He balked at the repugnant surrounding odor and, distracted, he was afraid he might throw up.

A grygot slammed into his shield with a raspy squeal then collapsed as a dart flew between Jon's legs into its side. Jon hurried forward and created a path by pushing the smaller grygots away with his shield.

His body slammed into a rough wood panel. He tugged at a rusty iron pull jutting into his right side. The door remained fixed like a heavy granite gravestone.

Oh no, it's really stuck.

A grygot bumped into his back and its razor teeth tore into his thigh. He turned around and smacked at it with the shield. Immediately, two Keepers materialized from the mist to fight it back.

Jon's leg stung and his anger grew. He dropped the shield and grabbed the door pull with both hands. Focusing his mind as Jharliss had taught him, he jerked the door toward his chest with all his might. He imagined it greased at the hinges and opening easily. It creaked and opened a crack.

This is encouraging. A glimmer of hope rose in his chest.

He set his right foot against the wall for leverage and yanked the rusty pull one more time. This time, the door snapped open and slammed into the rock wall. The impact of the iron pull forced a spray of rock chips to clatter to the floor.

Jon shot a quick glance back to assess his grygot danger. At this moment, nothing approached. Throughout the tunnel, the action had significantly quieted except for a few muted pops as darts hit the crusty hides of the remaining grygots. Moans from Keepers filtered out from thinning fog and Reil rang out orders for the treatment of the injured.

Jon slipped his hand into his pouch one last time. Orlo nipped it. "Go lad, go. The Amara is intact." Jon took a very deep breath and slid through the open doorway into thick blackness.

TEMPLE PRINCE

Nine

Kaz

A single thought cycled through Jon's head. *"You don't want to be here. You really don't want to be here."* The words repeated over and over with a life of their own.

He didn't want to be there, but he remembered Orlo's words about intentions and making choices. *The choices we make now determine our future.* Those words sustained him as fear swelled to cut off his breath. He swallowed the hard lump in his throat as he stared at the indistinct outline of Kaz's enormous bulk filling the lower part of another great chamber. The mountain remained still except for slow coarse breathing. Its sides heaved and its large nostrils flared as they expelled each breath.

Kaz is still sleeping. Jon sidled around a concave wall at his left for a better view. As he approached the head he leaned back against the wall to find the best shot.

The monster's long jaw pressed flat against the floor. Spiky batwing earflaps folded back above narrow cheeks. Behind the head, the brackish skin covered a warty rippled body. A black halo of death wrapped around Kaz's body and blended back into dark recesses. Jon's nose twitched from a rotting carcass odor wafting through the air.

A massive tail trailed along the floor and wound back to tuck its tip under the midsection where a ridged chest full of large open pores oozed yellowish slimy stuff to pool on the floor. One foot, resembling a talon and ending in elongated and pointed black curved nails, angled away from the mass of body.

T–Rex was a child's toy next to Kaz.

The longer Jon stared at Kaz, the more he felt the flood of negative sensations surrounding it: chaos; anti–order; pain for pleasure; pure greed; ugliness in mind, body, and heart; doubt and fear; addiction. This converged into one stinking idea bomb and sickened him.

Jon grieved that such a creature existed. The grief grew to despair when he knew that human weakness allowed an entry to evil and assured Kaz's success. He closed his eyes and knew he had made the right choice in helping to keep this creature from mixing with his world. Although people sometimes acted in a negative way, they still could make choices. Kaz's presence doomed that ability. Jon saw this knowledge with total clarity though he could not have explained it. His understanding came from experiencing the monster's presence. Jon felt this truth in his innermost being. Humans didn't stand a chance against an evil they had no ability to detect.

"Hurry Jon. Proceed with your task." The urging came from his pouch.

Jon lifted his sling and placed a vial into the strap while he searched for the best target. The underside openings turned away at an angle beneath the sleeping giant making them difficult to reach. The head lay close except the mouth remained clamped into a tight line. Jon chose the huge nostril.

He stepped away from the wall to quietly and smoothly draw back his arm to aim. Keeping both arms at a steady level, his fingers let go of the elastic strap. The vial released and sailed directly into the center of the pulsating nostril.

A hit. Jon sighed in relief, his job finished. *Not bad!*

At the next intake of breath, the monstrous head of Kaz jerked backwards followed by a terrifying flash of muscle movement. Kaz rose to the great height of the chamber. Its head brushed the ceiling. Then it spun around a quarter turn and arched its long neck to Jon's eye level to scorch his soul with penetrating eyes.

A faint smile flipped up at the corners of the dragon's mouth. The yellow slime oozed like lava from the exposed underside openings.

Jon heard the words, "Focus. Focus" coming from somewhere. His pouch? Jon's confusion muddled his concentration.

He shook with terror despite of an effort to stay calm. When the dragon drew a pointy claw up to his chest, Jon jumped back and slammed his body against the rock wall.

Crunch! Amber liquid formed a dark circle at the bottom of the pouch after the sickening sound of glass cracking. Amara drizzled out at the corner seam. Jon panicked.

Kaz drew back and let out an enormous roar. The cavern amplified and reverberated the sound until the walls turned to shivering jelly.

Then he *snorted!* Absolute dread poured into Jon as the first glass vial popped out of the huge nostril and smashed into the wall over his head. It shattered into thin shards. The precious amber liquid dripped in rivulets toward the floor.

Kaz roared again. Cracking walls responded by hurling chunks of rock through the air. Jon's legs rooted into the surrounding rock. The cavern's wooden door stood a hundred miles away.

Kaz drew its head back as if to strike viper style.

Is this the end?

Jon decided not to stand there and die. Instead, he'd finish his task and try to escape.

"You can get everyone in the world, but you're not getting me," his mind screamed at the dragon.

Jon still could not force his feet to move, but managed to shove his shaking arm into the open pouch. To his relief, his fingers reached the smooth undamaged globe of the third vial wedged into the bottom corner underneath a silent Orlo. Soaked with Amara, Orlo lay motionless.

Was Orlo dead?

Jon had no time to worry. Kaz moved toward him so Jon slapped the vial into the sling. He aimed toward the hideous head and drew the elastic cord back in one continuous motion. The vial snapped through the air and smacked Kaz right in the middle of the ridge forming his brow line. When the fragile glass broke, its contents dripped into a blinking yellow eye. The golden Amara stung Kaz. Surprised and taken aback, the monster paused.

Then he pulled his head back and released another tremendous angry roar. Jon seized this moment to sprint toward the chamber's entryway. He broke into full flight and slammed the door behind him. When he reached the first bend of the tunnel he stopped for a quick moment to catch his breath. The small door remained closed and trapped Kaz. With no other exit visible Jon thought, *I'm safe. It's done.* He could do nothing more.

Eerie silence in the tunnel echoed the unexpected stillness coming from Kaz's chamber. The Keepers and the grygots had vanished leaving broken darts and fragments of torn clothing scattered on the floor. Drugged grygots melded into it, dark rocks among splotches of dried blood. The Keepers had removed any evidence of casualties. Jon hoped there had been none.

He pulled Orlo from the pouch and jiggled the sleeping stone.

"Orlo. Orlo, wake up!"

Orlo didn't respond to the hard shaking. Jon could not know that years would pass before the stone woke from his drugged slumber.

Kaz's chamber trembled. The small door wiggled. Jon suspected the Amara might not affect Kaz right away. *Time to put a safe distance between us.* He must find Jharliss for help in finding his way out since Orlo remained still.

Screeching came from the behind the wooden door. The hinges squealed and wailed. The door's wood bowed toward him. Crack. Crack. Craaaaaackkkk!!! The door blasted away from its hinges. Chunks of wood sailed in every direction and ricocheted off the floor and walls like missiles.

The tip of a bumpy nose appeared in the irregular space where the door once stood. Then two squeezed nostrils appeared. Kaz shoved the front part of its head through the doorway. Slime oozed out along the sides. Flesh melted through the rock edges and solidified once inside the tunnel. Kaz compressed his muscles and pushed out further.

When Kaz's eyes emerged Jon turned and scrambled through the floor's debris. The space between him and the gleaming eyes narrowed. Kaz birthed himself through the tunnel with amazing speed! Jon gained distance when Kaz stopped to compress, but then lost ground as the creature pushed forward.

Hot fiery breath licked Jon's heels as he struggled up through the steep incline to the opening where the bridges stood. Or once stood, he saw to his dismay. The brand new bridges hung in shreds of rope and broken boards. So, Jon scurried through the only passageway left open—straight toward the Chamber of the Souls.

TEMPLE PRINCE

Ten

Transfiguration

A blast of commotion rushed at Jon from the chamber opening. He sprinted out onto the high walkway and looked at the great chamber's spectacle with alarm. A mad carnival replaced the earlier orderly procession. Souls no longer understood how to move ahead to the transition wall and their frustrated wails echoed through the tunnels.

There must be a way out of this mess.

Fallen rock blocked the pathway to Jharliss' chamber. Jon looked around for another escape route.

The ferret's familiar squeak called him to the top of a steep trail that Jon had not noticed on his earlier pass along the ridge. The trail switched back and forth across the steep cliff to stop at the river. Jon followed her lead. It took a long time for them to reach the flat landing at its base. A dinghy with small oars waited at the shore. Jon's intuition told him that the Keepers used it to repair the bridges. It provided a tight fit with his larger size.

Sweat broke out on his forehead and his body felt as if he were burning. Was it from exertion traversing the cliff? Or was he getting sick? He felt dizzy, weak, and hot. He snatched up a staff lying near the boat and jumped in behind the ferret. The staff found hard bottom, and he wedged the boat away from the shore. Jon switched to the oars after a few feet when he hit the water's greater depth.

Rock exploded from overhead as Kaz burst out from the tunnel into the Souls' Chamber. Shrill screaming erupted as palpable waves of negative intent rolled off the dragon to soak the cavern's inhabitants. They zigzagged around in the river in a frantic state.

The ghost of a matronly English woman called out as she pointed, "We must be in hell. There is the devil."

Kaz squished himself out onto the curving ledge with several strong pulses and drew himself up to full size. He announced his arrival with loud shocking roars that increased the dismay of the agitated ghosts. They fled back to the far bank, where they had first entered the cavern. Here they pressed into one massive horde with each form blending into the one next to it.

Jon pulled his oars hard to get to the opposite shore. But the river stretched wide at this point and the rising fury of the water slowed his progress. Kaz fixed his gaze on the small boat.

Then fortune turned its wheel. The enraged dragon teetered forward, then backward as the sleeping potion took effect. Kaz clung to the edge of the high walkway with great talons curled around the rock. He lunged forward, caught himself, and rocked back. The arc of his sway became slower, larger, and more irregular. His eyes lost their luster. With one last great roar, Kaz slipped forward and tumbled toward the midst of the confused souls. Havoc followed.

Jon watched everything with rising hope. *Maybe the Amara was working!*

But before Kaz reached the surface of the water, the mighty creature spread its wings outward and swooped way up in a circular movement. As its belly reached the apex of the circle, fire blasted out of its mouth toward the top of the cavern to form a glowing ring in the heated rock.

Jon approached the middle of the river. Ferocious waves lapped the boat's sides and threatened to swamp the small craft. Abandoning his oars, he gripped both sides of the boat to keep from being thrown out. It bobbed up and down in the frenzied river.

In the meantime, the ferret had flattened herself into the bottom under the seat. Now the rising water inside the boat forced her from that spot. She jumped onto the seat beside Jon and pushed her lithe body between his torso and his arm.

Large waves of angry water splashed over the sides of the boat, drenching them both. The ferret was slipping away. Jon tried to squeeze her to his body with his elbow so he could hold her firmly. He feared letting go of the boat's sides.

A bigger wave hit them and the ferret abandoned ship. She undulated through whitecaps back to the moss–covered landing and climbed to safety.

The water from the River of Deeds soaked Jon to the bone. The wet rags of his clothes stuck to his body.

Funny, the water tickles. Something isn't right.

His skin crawled. When he let go of the boat's sides and briskly rubbed his arms and legs, multicolored streams of steam spiraled away from his body. *How odd!* A few streams appeared murky and dark. Others flew off in captivating bright hues of pink, blue, and gold. A voice drew his attention.

Jharliss! "Stay centered."

"Where are you Jharliss?"

A shadow smothered the boat. Jon looked straight up. Kaz hovered ten feet above, with mouth open, ready to scorch Jon and boat together.

Jon scrambled to his feet, intending to dive and swim to the opposite shore. A wave knocked him back to the bottom where he smashed his elbow on the seat.

He tried to get up again but, before he moved, Kaz lurched sideways. A point of bright light had appeared out of nowhere and pushed the dragon aside. Kaz flinched and wobbled. It swung around to face the tiny star of light. The light flickered and grew to the size of a basketball while emanating rings of rainbow colors. The rings spread out over the cavern and illuminated the faces of the ghost horde. They hushed.

Kaz straightened himself in mid air and, for seconds, the world disappeared into a bright nothingness. Then a baby cried out.

The orb of light sent fingers into the far reaches of the cavern. A shape formed as the light folded and spread. The eyes and head of Jharliss emerged within a brilliant halo.

She moved forward to pierce the chest of the great beast. Unending blackness poured out of his heart. When Jharliss' face appeared superimposed over the ugliness of Kaz, Jon supposed delirium had set in.

What a strange sight! Her radiance shone out from the top of the hideous body. Then she shot up to the ceiling and Kaz's face cleared again.

At once, Kaz dropped toward the river. It tried to extend its wings, but they folded back to its sides. The massive dragon plunged into the River of Deeds head first. As soon as the first bit of its nose penetrated the surface, the water erupted into frothy bubbles that gurgled around the sinking flesh. A noxious odor filled the cave.

Jon shielded his eyes from the dazzling radiance of Jharliss' glowing orb as he watched the tip of Kaz's enormous barbed tail sink into the water. No sooner had the tail disappeared from sight than the nose of Kaz emerged from between two large waves. Jon's heart rose to his throat. *It's not over!*

Thinking pummeled his brain. "What is without is within." Isn't that what Orlo told him?

What is within?

His body burned. His throat hurt along with the muscles in

his legs and arms. Pain seared across the crown of his head. His back ached.

What is within? Within me?

A spot of recognition surfaced. Jon connected a piece of himself with a piece of the dragon. *Why, I feel him inside me! And Jharliss too!*

The gargantuan apparition of Kaz floated up from the churning water. Its eyes had changed. They had softened and widened. The face muscles relaxed. Most astonishing, the dragon's color lightened to match the whitish hue of the surrounding ghosts. The translucent shape turned to face the sparkling wall of transition and floated placidly forward as the orb containing Jharliss pulsated overhead.

Musical tones from no apparent source penetrated the chamber and echoed off the walls. Their volume increased as Kaz's form blended halfway into the transition wall under the ridge. A low murmuring arose from the observant pack of ghosts. After a brief but tense pause, the last half of Kaz filtered through to the Inner World.

Now the orb threw out blinding light with heightened colors that bounced off the walls in the cavernous chamber and passed through the horde of souls. They floated toward the orb attracted by the light. Soothing calm spread out in wispy streaks and filtered through their shapes.

Jon's eyes narrowed to thin slits as he succumbed to exhaustion. They widened when his name came from the orb in musical and lilting tones.

"Fare thee well. We will meet again, Jon. You performed exceedingly well."

The orb sailed straight into the water and, at once, Jharliss' resplendent magnificence erupted from radiating circles on the surface. She never looked at Jon or the ghosts.

Instead, she floated straight into the wall of transition with her head flung back and arms outstretched at her side. A large group of trailing spirits blended in close behind pulled in her wake.

A moment of realization flashed through Jon's mind just before he passed out and slid to the boat's bottom. In that instant, he knew, beyond any shadow of doubt, that Jharliss had foreseen this. She *knew* he would not succeed in putting Kaz to sleep. He had functioned as a lure to bring Kaz to the River of Deeds and to Jharliss. The complete transformation of Kaz provided a permanent solution to their problem.

Eleven

Home Again

Jon opened his eyes. Was he dreaming again?

A familiar face beamed at him breaking his disorientation. Jon smiled back weakly and puckered his chapped lips together to speak. His mind groped for the source of his misery.

"Where am I?" The sound came out of his mouth in a froggy croak.

"You're at Aunt Kate's house," Jules replied. He was happy to see life returning to Jon.

"We're having repairs made to our house due to quake damage. So we're camping out with your aunt for a couple weeks. You've been a sick boy with a bad bout of encephalitis. You had us worried, including Doctor Bob. For the life of me, I don't understand how you picked up that bug here in the mountains after this long dry spell. The disease control people are so worked up they set mosquito traps everywhere. Our search party found you outside what looked like a collapsed bear cave. You suffered from severe dehydration and have run a fever for several days. Doctor Bob pumped you full of fluids and tried three different antibiotics before we found one that worked."

"We'd been looking for you for over a week with no leads. Then the search party heard an animal making a huge ruckus. It looked like a weasel. Stasos took off chasing it and the rest of us followed to catch him."

"You remember Fred Gossmeyer, the naturalist from the university? He thought it might be a near extinct ferret but he didn't get a good look at it before it ran away. Anyway, when we went to get Stasos, we found you unconscious on the ground. I was so relieved to find you. You'd been gone so long we were afraid something terrible had happened to you."

"Is mom here? And Andy?"

"Yes, Jon. We're here. We're fine." His mother answered. Jon turned his head. When his eyes cleared he saw the rest of his family surrounding the bed.

His father continued, "We missed you so much and we love you. But don't try to talk now son. We can talk later. We want you to get better. You need your rest if you're going to be one hundred percent of your old self in time for our summer vacation."

He tousled Jon's hair before they all quietly filed out of his bedroom.

Stasos visited Jon next. He pushed the door open with his nose. Putting both front paws on the bed, his sloppy tongue licked the feet that stuck out under Jon's blanket. Stasos's tail turned into an unstoppable metronome.

"Yikes. Stasos. OK. Enough!"

It's so good to be home. Jon snuggled under his blanket and dozed into a dozen dreams. He dreamed the first dream of a beautiful lady with red hair and kind eyes who would continue to haunt his sleep the rest of his life. Just as he called out her name, she faded away. Another dream followed with a weird talking stone. He thought he knew something about it, but his fever kept him from concentrating.

Jon slept off and on. He vaguely remembered little people dragging him through a tunnel and to the mouth of a cave. But now he wasn't sure who they were, or if he had dreamed them. In the far reaches of his mind something important had happened— something that changed him and everything that existed in a permanent way. He figured he must have really been sick.

Jon grew stronger in the days that followed. He recuperated back to his old self. Something inside had changed though. He no longer felt impatient with Andrea. Those girlish ways that irritated him earlier amused him now. Little things didn't bother him as they did before his sickness. Even his aunt commented on the change. She said he'd 'matured.'

He took an interest in his mother's garden and spent many hours helping her weed the beds, without her asking. In his mind, he 'saw' little green men next to him tending to the needs of the plants. He questioned his mother constantly. What makes the plants grow? Do vegetables make you healthier? Do different soils affect the plants' growths? And since her ancestors included a long line of gardeners, she provided the right answers.

"I think you are a future botanist," she remarked one day.

Nancy appreciated his new interest in more adult activities. She supposed he was growing up. However, she worried about young people these days. They appeared self–indulgent and many held little regard for others. Was this from television's influence? Now she thought of her son with bursting pride.

Jon continued to race in competitions. By the next year he won a regional award for his achievement in track. Coach Coleman told him that his 'concentration' inspired the other runners.

Jon continued his interest in plants right up to the time he chose a career—in Botany, of course!

His most important change showed up in the way he approached decisions. He pondered a choice for hours and projected different outcomes. In many ways, he lived a more serious life. Perhaps he had learned which things were important and where you could choose your focus. He now forgot about the little things that would not make a true difference in his life.

As for his family, they never contended with problems with their home again. The quakes stopped as mysteriously as they began. The spacious log home would stay in the family for three generations. Jon and Andrea grew up holding happy childhood memories. Life unfolded in a normal and pleasant manner for the Pryce family.

That is until the day Jon met *the Sprite* in his mother's garden and his next adventure began.

JONATHAN PRYCE AND THE MAGIC STONE